"I had only to read the two opening sentences of THE GHOST WRITER to realize—with a long sigh of anticipated pleasure—that I was once again in the hands of a superbly endowed storyteller.... The voice that Philip Roth has developed for his first-person narrations—notably PORTNOY'S COMPLAINT, MY LIFE AS A MAN and, recently, THE PROFESSOR OF DESIRE—is surely one of the most distinctive and supple in contemporary American fiction. It is a voice of remarkable range, accommodating sentences of almost Jamesian convolution and allusiveness with sudden ejaculations of street language, comic hyperbole with ironic understatement, tones of melancholy self-deprecation with bursts of satiric glee. It is a voice that inspires in me, at least, confidence that what follows will be entertaining, sharply observed, possibly a bit nasty, almost certainly provocative."

—ROBERT TOWERS
The New York Times Book Review
(front page)

PHILIP ROTH

The Ghost Writer

FAWCETT CREST • NEW YORK

For MILAN KUNDERA

The Ghost Writer

1

Maestro

It was the last daylight hour of a December afternoon more than twenty years ago—I was twenty-three, writing and publishing my first short stories, and like many a *Bildungsroman* hero before me, already contemplating my own massive *Bildungsroman*—when I arrived at his hideaway to meet the great man. The clapboard farmhouse was at the end of an unpaved road twelve hundred feet up in the Berkshires, yet the figure who emerged from the study to bestow a ceremonious greeting wore a gabardine suit, a

knitted blue tie clipped to a white shirt by an
unadorned silver clasp, and well-brushed
ministerial black shoes that made me think
of him stepping down from a shoeshine stand
rather than from the high altar of art. Before
I had composure enough to notice the com-
manding, autocratic angle at which he held
his chin, or the regal, meticulous, rather
dainty care he took to arrange his clothes
before sitting—to notice anything, really,
other than that I had miraculously made it
from my unliterary origins to here, to him—
my impression was that E. I. Lonoff looked
more like the local superintendent of schools
than the region's most original storyteller
since Melville and Hawthorne.

Not that the New York gossip about him
should have led me to expect anything more
grand. When I had recently raised his name
before the jury at my first Manhattan publishing party—I'd arrived, excited as a star-
let, on the arm of an elderly editor—Lonoff
was almost immediately disposed of by the
wits on hand as though it were comical that
a Jew of his generation, an immigrant child
to begin with, should have married the scion
of an old New England family and lived all
these years "in the country"—that is to say, in
the *goyish* wilderness of birds and trees

10

where America began and long ago had ended. However, since everybody else of renown I mentioned at the party also seemed slightly amusing to those in the know, I had been skeptical about their satiric description of the famous rural recluse. In fact, from what I saw at that party, I could begin to understand why hiding out twelve hundred feet up in the mountains with just the birds and the trees might not be a bad idea for a writer, Jewish or not.

The living room he took me into was neat, cozy, and plain: a large circular hooked rug, some slipcovered easy chairs, a worn sofa, a long wall of books, a piano, a phonograph, an oak library table systematically stacked with journals and magazines. Above the white wainscoting, the pale-yellow walls were bare but for half a dozen amateur watercolors of the old farmhouse in different seasons. Beyond the cushioned windowseats and the colorless cotton curtains tied primly back I could see the bare limbs of big dark maple trees and fields of driven snow. Purity. Serenity. Simplicity. Seclusion. All one's concentration and flamboyance and originality reserved for the grueling, exalted, transcendent calling. I looked around and I thought, This is how I will live.

After directing me to one of a pair of easy chairs beside the fireplace, Lonoff removed the fire screen and peered in to be sure the draft was open. With a wooden match he lighted the kindling that apparently had been laid there in anticipation of our meeting. Then he placed the fire screen back into position as precisely as though it were being fitted into a groove in the hearth. Certain that the logs had caught—satisfied that he had successfully ignited a fire without endangering the two-hundred-year-old house or its inhabitants—he was ready at last to join me. With hands that were almost ladylike in the swiftness and delicacy of their movements, he hiked the crease in each trouser leg and took his seat. He moved with a notable lightness for such a large, heavyset man.

"How would you prefer to be addressed?" asked Emanuel Isidore Lonoff. "As Nathan, Nate, or Nat? Or have you another preference entirely?" Friends and acquaintances called him Manny, he informed me, and I should do the same. "That will make conversation easier."

I doubted that, but I smiled to indicate that no matter how light-headed it was bound to leave me, I would obey. The master then proceeded to undo me further by asking to hear something from me about my life. Needless to say, there wasn't much to report about my life in 1956—certainly not, as I saw it, to someone so knowing and deep. I had been raised by doting parents in a Newark neighborhood neither rich nor poor; I had a younger brother who was said to idolize me; at a good local high school and an excellent college I had performed as generations of my forebears had expected me to; subsequently I had served in the Army, stationed just an hour from home, writing public-information handouts for a Fort Dix major, even while the massacre for which my carcass had been drafted was being bloodily concluded in Korea. Since my discharge I had been living and writing in a five-flight walk-up off lower Broadway, characterized by my girl friend, when she came to share the place and fix it up a little, as the home of an unchaste monk.

To support myself I crossed the river to New Jersey three days a week to a job I'd held on and off since my first summer in college, when I'd answered an ad promising high commissions to aggressive salesmen. At eight each morning our crew was driven to some New Jersey mill town to sell magazine subscriptions door-to-door, and at six we were picked up outside a designated saloon and

driven back to downtown Newark by the over-
seer, McElroy. He was a spiffy rummy with
a hairline mustache who never tired of warn-
ing us—two high-minded boys who were putting away their earnings for an education,
and three listless old-timers, pale, puffy men
wrecked by every conceivable misfortune—
not to fool with the housewives we found
alone at home in their curlers: you could get
your neck broken by an irate husband, you
could be set up for walloping blackmail, you
could catch any one of fifty leprous varieties
of clap, and what was more, there were only
so many hours in the day. "Either get laid,"
he coldly advised us, "or sell *Silver Screen*.
Take your pick." "Mammon's Moses" we two
college boys called him. Since no housewife
ever indicated a desire to invite me into the
hallway to so much as rest my feet—and I
was vigilantly on the lookout for lascivious-
ness flaring up in any woman of any age who
seemed even half willing to listen to me from
behind her screen door—I of necessity chose
perfection of the work rather than the life,
and by the end of each long day of canvassing
had ten to twenty dollars in commissions to
my credit and an unblemished future still
before me. It was only a matter of weeks since
I had relinquished this unhallowed life—and

the girl friend in the five-flight walkup, whom I no longer loved—and, with the help of the distinguished New York editor, had been welcomed for the winter months as a communicant at the Quahsay Colony, the rural artists' retreat across the state line from Lonoff's mountain.

From Quahsay I had sent Lonoff the literary quarterlies that had published my stories—four so far—along with a letter telling him how much he had meant to me when I came upon his work "some years ago" in college. In the same breath I mentioned coming upon his "kinsmen" Chekhov and Gogol, and went on to reveal in other unmistakable ways just how serious a literary fellow I was—and, hand in hand with that, how young. But then nothing I had ever written put me in such a sweat as that letter. Everything undeniably true struck me as transparently false as soon as I wrote it down, and the greater the effort to be sincere, the worse it went. I finally sent him the tenth draft and then tried to stick my arm down the throat of the mailbox to extract it.

I wasn't doing any better in the plain and cozy living room with my autobiography. Because I could not bring myself to utter even the mildest obscenity in front of Lonoff's early

American mantelpiece, my imitation of Mr. McElroy—a great favorite among my friends—didn't really have much to recommend it. Nor could I speak easily of all McElroy had warned us against, or begin to mention how tempted I would have been to yield, if opportunity had only knocked. You would have thought, listening to my bowdlerized version of what was a tepid enough little life history, that rather than having received a warm and gracious letter from the famous writer inviting me to come and spend a pleasant evening in his house, I had made this journey to plead a matter of utmost personal urgency before the most stringent of inquisitors, and that if I made one wrong move, something of immeasurable value to me would be lost forever.

Which was pretty much the case, even if I didn't completely understand as yet how desperate I was for his recognition, and why. Far from being nonplused by my bashful, breathless delivery—out of character though it was for me in those confident years—I should have been surprised to find that I wasn't down on the hooked rug, supplicating at his feet. For I had come, you see, to submit myself for candidacy as nothing less than E. I. Lonoff's spiritual son, to petition for his moral sponsorship and to win, if I could, the magical protection of his advocacy and his love. Of course, I had a loving father of my own, whom I could ask the world of any day of the week, but my father was a foot doctor and not an artist, and lately we had been having serious trouble in the family because of a new story of mine. He was so bewildered by what I had written that he had gone running to *his* moral mentor, a certain Judge Leopold Wapter, to get the judge to get his son to see the light. As a result, after two decades of a more or less unbroken amiable conversation, we had not been speaking for nearly five weeks now, and I was off and away seeking patriarchal validation elsewhere.

And not just from a father who was an artist instead of a foot doctor, but from the most famous literary ascetic in America, that giant of patience and fortitude and selflessness who, in the twenty-five years between his first book and his sixth (for which he was given a National Book Award that he quietly declined to accept), had virtually no readership or recognition, and invariably would be dismissed, if and when he was even mentioned, as some quaint remnant of the Old World ghetto, an out-of-step folklorist pathetically oblivious of the major currents of literature and society. Hardly anyone knew

17

who he was or where actually he lived, and for a quarter of a century almost nobody cared. Even among his readers there had been some who thought that E. I. Lonoff's fantasies about Americans had been written in Yiddish somewhere inside czarist Russia before he supposedly died there (as, in fact, his father had nearly perished) from injuries suffered in a pogrom. What was so admirable to me was not only the tenacity that had kept him writing his own kind of stories all that time but that having been "discovered" and popularized, he refused all awards and degrees, declined membership in all honorary institutions, granted no public interviews, and chose not to be photographed, as though to associate his face with his fiction were a ridiculous irrelevancy.

The only photograph anyone in the reading public had ever seen was the watery sepia portrait which had appeared in 1927 on an inside jacket flap of *It's Your Funeral*: the handsome young artist with the lyrical almond eyes and the dark prow of a paramour's pompadour and the kissable, expressive underlip. So different was he now, not just because of jowls and a belly and the white-fringed, bald cranium but as a human type altogether, that I thought (once I began to be able to think) it had to be something more ruthless than time that accounted for the metamorphosis: it would have to be Lonoff himself. Other than the full, glossy eyebrows and the vaguely heavenward tilt of the willful chin, there was really nothing at all to identify him, at fifty-six, with the photo of the passionate, forlorn, shy Valentino who, in the decade lorded over by the young Hemingway and Fitzgerald, had written a collection of short stories about wandering Jews unlike anything written before by any Jew who had wandered into America.

In fact, my own first reading through Lonoff's canon—as an orthodox college atheist and highbrow-in-training—had done more to make me realize how much I was still my family's Jewish offspring than anything I had carried forward to the University of Chicago from childhood Hebrew lessons, or mother's kitchen, or the discussions I used to hear among my parents and our relatives about the perils of intermarriage, the problem of Santa Claus, and the injustice of medical-school quotas (quotas that, as I understood early on, accounted for my father's career in chiropody and his ardent lifelong support of the B'nai B'rith Anti-Defamation League). As a grade-school kid I could already debate these intricate issues with anyone (and did, when called upon); by the time I left for Chicago, however, my passion had been pretty well spent and I was as ready as an adolescent could be to fall headlong for Robert Hutchins' Humanities One. But then, along with tens of thousands of others, I discovered E. I. Lonoff, whose fiction seemed to me a response to the same burden of exclusion and confinement that still weighed upon the lives of those who had raised me, and that had informed our relentless household obsession with the status of the Jews. The pride inspired in my parents by the establishment in 1948 of a homeland in Palestine that would gather in the unmurdered remnant of European Jewry was, in fact, not so unlike what welled up in me when I first came upon Lonoff's thwarted, secretive, imprisoned souls, and realized that out of everything humbling from which my own striving, troubled father had labored to elevate us all, a literature of such dour wit and poignancy could be shamelessly conceived. To me it was as though the hallucinatory strains in Gogol had been filtered through the humane skepticism of Chekhov to nourish the country's first "Russian" writer. Or so I argued in the college essay where I "analyzed" Lonoff's style but

kept to myself an explication of the feelings
of kinship that his stories had revived in me
for our own largely Americanized clan, mon-
eyless immigrant shopkeepers to begin with,
who'd carried on a shtetl life ten minutes'
walk from the pillared banks and gargoyled
insurance cathedrals of downtown Newark;
and what is more, feelings of kinship for our
pious, unknown ancestors, whose Galician
tribulations had been only a little less foreign
to me, while growing up securely in New Jersey, than Abraham's in the Land of Canaan.
With his vaudevillian's feel for legend and
landscape (a Chaplin, I said of Lonoff in my
senior paper, who seized upon just the right
prop to bring an entire society and its outlook
to life); with his "translated" English to lend
a mildly ironic flavor to even the most com-
monplace expression; with his cryptic, muted,
dreamy resonance, the sense given by such
little stories of saying so much—well, I had
proclaimed, who in American literature was
like him?

The typical hero of a Lonoff story—the hero
who came to mean so much to bookish Americans in the mid-fifties, the hero who, some
ten years after Hitler, seemed to say something new and wrenching to Gentiles about
Jews, and to Jews about themselves, and to

readers and writers of that recuperative decade generally about the ambiguities of prudence and the anxieties of disorder, about life-hunger, life-bargains, and life-terror in their most elementary manifestations—Lonoff's hero is more often than not a nobody from nowhere, away from a home where he is not missed, yet to which he must return without delay. His celebrated blend of sympathy and pitilessness (monumentalized as "Lonovian" by *Time*—after decades of ignoring him completely) is nowhere more stunning than in the stories where the bemused isolate steels himself to be carried away, only to discover that his meticulous thoughtfulness has caused him to wait a little too long to do anyone any good, or that acting with bold and uncharacteristic impetuosity, he has totally misjudged what had somehow managed to entice him out of his manageable existence, and as a result has made everything worse.

The grimmest, funniest, and most unsettling stories of all, where the pitiless author seems to me to teeter just at the edge of self-impalement, were written during the brief period of his literary glory (for he died in 1961 of a bone-marrow disease; and when Oswald shot Kennedy and the straitlaced bulwark gave way to the Gargantuan banana republic, his fiction, and the authority it granted to all that is prohibitive in life, began rapidly losing "relevance" for a new generation of readers). Rather than cheering him up, Lonoff's eminence seemed to strengthen his dourest imaginings, confirming for him visions of terminal restraint that might have seemed insufficiently supported by personal experience had the world denied him its rewards right down to the end. Only when a little of the coveted bounty was finally his for the asking—only when it became altogether clear just how stupefyingly unsuited he was to have and to hold anything other than his art—was he inspired to write that brilliant cycle of comic parables (the stories "Revenge," "Lice," "Indiana," "Eppes Essen," and "Adman") in which the tantalized hero does not move to act *at all*—the tiniest impulse toward amplitude or self-surrender, let alone intrigue or adventure, peremptorily extinguished by the ruling triumvirate of Sanity, Responsibility, and Self-Respect, assisted handily by their devoted underlings: the timetable, the rainstorm, the headache, the busy signal, the traffic jam, and most loyal of all, the last-minute doubt.

Did I sell any magazines other than *Photoplay* and *Silver Screen*? Did I use the same line at every door or adapt my sales pitch to the customer? How did I account for my success as a salesman? What did I think people were after who subscribed to these insipid magazines? Was the work boring? Did anything unusual ever happen while I was prowling neighborhoods I knew nothing about? How many crews like Mr. McElroy's were there in New Jersey? How could the company afford to pay me three dollars for each subscription I sold? Had I ever been to Hackensack? What was it like?

It was difficult to believe that what I was doing merely to support myself until I might begin to live as he did could possibly be of interest to E. I. Lonoff. He was a courteous man, obviously, and he was trying his best to put me at ease, but I was thinking, even as I gave my all to his cross-examination, that it wasn't going to be long before he came up with a way of getting rid of me before dinner.

"I wish I knew that much about selling magazines," he said.

To indicate that it was all right with me if I was being condescended to and that I would understand if I was soon asked to leave, I went red.

"I wish," he said, "I knew that much about anything. I've written fantasy for thirty years. Nothing happens to me."

It was here that the striking girl-woman appeared before me—just as he had aired, in faintly discernible tones of self-disgust, this incredible lament and I was trying to grasp it. Nothing happened to him? Why, genius had happened to him, art had happened to him, the man was a visionary!

Lonoff's wife, the white-haired woman who had instantly removed herself after letting me into the house, had pushed open the door of the study across the foyer from the living room, and there she was, hair dark and profuse, eyes pale—gray or green—and with a high prominent oval forehead that looked like Shakespeare's. She was seated on the carpet amid a pile of papers and folders, swathed in a "New Look" tweed skirt—by now a very old, outmoded look in Manhattan—and a large, loose-fitting, white wool sweater; her legs were drawn demurely up beneath the expanse of skirt and her gaze was fixed on something that was clearly elsewhere. Where had I seen that severe dark

beauty before? Where but in a portrait by
Velázquez? I remembered the 1927 photograph of Lonoff—"Spanish" too in its way—
and immediately I assumed that she was his
daughter. Immediately I assumed more than
that. Mrs. Lonoff had not even set the tray
down on the carpet beside her before I saw
myself married to the *infanta* and living in
a little farmhouse of our own not that far
away. Only how old was she if Mama was
feeding her cookies while she finished her
homework on Daddy's floor? With that face,
whose strong bones looked to me to have been
worked into alignment by a less guileless
sculptor than nature—with that face she
must be more than twelve. Though if not, I
could wait. That idea appealed to me even
more than the prospect of a marriage here in
the living room in spring. Showed strength
of character, I thought. But what would the
famous father think? He of course wouldn't
need to be reminded of the solid Old Testament precedent for waiting seven years before making Miss Lonoff my bride; on the
other hand, how would he take it when he
saw me hanging around outside her high
school in my car?

Meanwhile, he was saying to me, "I turn
sentences around. That's my life. I write a

sentence and then I turn it around. Then I look at it and I turn it around again. Then I have lunch. Then I come back in and write another sentence. Then I read the two sentences over and turn them both around. Then I lie down on my sofa and think. Then I get up and throw them out and start from the beginning. And if I knock off from this routine for as long as a day, I'm frantic with boredom and a sense of waste. Sundays I have breakfast late and read the papers with Hope. Then we go for a walk in the hills, and I'm haunted by the loss of all that good time. I wake up Sunday mornings and I'm nearly crazy at the prospect of all those unusable hours. I'm restless, I'm bad-tempered, but she's a human being too, you see, so I go. To avoid trouble she makes me leave my watch at home. The result is that I look at my wrist instead. We're walking, she's talking, then I look at my wrist—and that generally does it, if my foul mood hasn't already. She throws in the sponge and we come home. And at home what is there to distinguish Sunday from Thursday? I sit back down at my little Olivetti and start looking at sentences and turning them around. And I ask myself, Why is there no way but this for me to fill my hours?"

By now Hope Lonoff had closed the study door and returned to her chores. Together Lonoff and I listened to her Mixmaster whirling in the kitchen. I didn't know what to say. The life he described sounded like paradise to me; that he could think to do nothing better with his time than turn sentences around seemed to me a blessing bestowed not only upon him but upon world literature. I wondered if perhaps I was supposed to be laughing, despite the deadpan delivery, at his description of his day, if it wasn't intended as mordant Lonovian comedy; though then again, if he meant it and was as depressed as he sounded, oughtn't I to remind him just who he was and how much he mattered to literate mankind? But how could he not know that?

The Mixmaster whirled and the fire popped and the wind blew and the trees groaned while I tried, at twenty-three, to think of how to dispel his gloom. His openness about himself, so at odds with his formal attire and his pedantic manner, had me as unnerved as anything else; it was hardly what I was accustomed to getting from people more than twice my age, even if what he said about himself was tinged with self-satire. Especially if it was tinged with self-satire.

"I wouldn't even try to write after my tea

any more if I knew what to do with myself for the rest of the afternoon." He explained to me that by three o'clock he no longer had the strength or the determination or even the desire to go on. But what else was there? If he played the violin or the piano, then he might have had some serious activity other than reading to occupy him when he was not writing. The problem with just listening to music was that if he sat alone with a record in the afternoon, he soon found himself turning the sentences around in his head and eventually wound up back at his desk again, skeptically looking at his day's work. Of course, to his great good fortune, there was Athene College. He spoke with devotion of the students in the two classes that he taught there. The little Stockbridge school had made a place for him on the faculty some twenty years before the rest of the academic world suddenly became interested, and for that he would always be grateful. But in truth, after so many years of teaching these bright and lively young women, both he and they, he found, had begun to repeat themselves a little.

"Why not take a sabbatical?" I was not a little thrilled, after all I had been through in my first fifteen minutes, to hear myself telling E. I. Lonoff how to live.

"I took a sabbatical. It was worse. We rented a flat in London for a year Then I had every day to write. Plus Hope being miserable because I wouldn't stop to go around with her to look at the buildings No—no more sabbaticals This way, at least two afternoons a week I have to stop, no questions asked. Besides, going to the college is the high point of my week I carry a briefcase I wear a ha I nod hello to people on the stairway I use a public toilet. Ask Hope I come home reeling from the pandemonium."

"Are there no children—of your own?"

The phone began ringing in the kitchen. Ignoring it, he informed me that the youngest of their three children had graduated from Wellesley several years before; he and his wife had been alone together now for more than six years.

So the girl isn't his daughter. Who is she then, being served snacks by his wife on the floor of his study? His concubine? Ridiculous, the word, the very idea, but there it was obscuring all other reasonable and worthy thoughts. Among the rewards you got for being a great artist was the concubinage of Velázquez princesses and the awe of young men like me. I felt at a loss again, having such ignoble expectations in the presence of my literary conscience—though weren't they just the kind of ignoble expectations that troubled the masters of renunciation in so many of Lonoff's short stories? Really, who knew better than E. I. Lonoff that it is not our high purposes alone that make us moving creatures, but our humble needs and cravings? Nonetheless, it seemed to me a good idea to keep my humble needs and cravings to myself.

The kitchen door opened a few inches and his wife said softly, "For you."

"Who is it? Not the genius again."

"Would I have said you were here?"

"You have to learn to tell people no. People like that make fifty calls a day. Inspiration strikes and they go for the phone."

"It's not him."

"He has the right wrong opinion on everything. A head full of ideas, every one of them stupid. Why does he hit me when he talks? Why must he understand everything? Stop fixing me up with intellectuals. I don't think fast enough."

"I've said I was sorry. And it's not him."

"Who is it?"

"Willis."

"Hope, I'm talking to Nathan here."

"I'm sorry. I'll tell him you're working."

"Don't use work as an excuse. I don't buy that."

"I can tell him you have a guest."

"Please," I said, meaning I was no one, not even a guest.

"All that wonder," said Lonoff to his wife. "Always so greatly moved. Always on the brink of tears. What is he so compassionate about all the time?"

"You," she said.

"All that sensitivity. Why does anybody want to be so sensitive?"

"He admires you," she said.

Buttoning his jacket, Lonoff rose to take the unwanted call. "Either it's the professional innocents," he explained to me, "or the deep thinkers."

I extended my sympathy with a shrug, wondering, of course, if my letter hadn't qualified me in both categories. Then I wondered again about the girl behind the study door. Does she live at the college or is she here with the Lonoffs on a visit from Spain? Would she ever be coming out of that study? If not, how do I go in? If not, how can I arrange to see her again by myself?

I must see you again.

I opened a magazine, the better to dispel my insidious daydreams and wait there like a thoughtful man of letters. Leafing through the pages, I came across an article about the Algerian political situation and another about the television industry, both of which had been underlined throughout. Read in sequence, the underlinings formed a perfect precis of each piece and would have served a schoolchild as excellent preparation for a report to his current-events class.

When Lonoff emerged—in under a minute—from the kitchen, he immediately undertook to explain about the *Harper's* in my hand. "My mind strays," he told me, rather as though I were a physician who had stopped by to ask about his strange and troubling new symptoms. "At the end of the page I try to summarize to myself what I've read and my mind is a blank—I've been sitting in my chair doing nothing. Of course, I have always read books with pen in hand, but now I find that if I don't, even while reading magazines, my attention is not on what's in front of me."

Here she appeared again. But what had seemed from a distance like beauty, pure and severe and simple, was more of a puzzle up close. When she crossed the foyer into the living room—entering just as Lonoff had ended his fastidious description of the disquieting affliction that came over him when he read magazines—I saw that the striking head had been conceived on a much grander and more ambitious scale than the torso. The bulky sweater and the pounds and pounds of tweed skirt did much, of course, to obscure the little of her there was, but mostly it was the drama of that face, combined with the softness and intelligence in her large pale eyes, that rendered all other physical attributes (excluding the heavy, curling hair) blurry and inconsequential. Admittedly, the rich calm of those eyes would have been enough to make me wilt with shyness, but that I couldn't return her gaze directly had also to do with this unharmonious relation between body and skull, and its implication, to me, of some early misfortune, of something vital lost or beaten down, and, by way of compensation, something vastly overdone. I thought of a trapped chick that could not get more than its beaked skull out of the encircling shell. I thought of those macrocephalic boulders the Easter Island heads. I thought of febrile patients on the verandas of Swiss sanatoria imbibing the magic-mountain air. But let me not exaggerate the pathos

34

and originality of my impressions, especially as they were subsumed soon enough in my unoriginal and irrepressible preoccupation. mostly I thought of the triumph it would be to kiss that face, and the excitement of her kissing me back

"Done," she announced to Lonoff, "for now "

His look of wistful solicitude made me wonder if she could be his *grand*daughter All at once he seemed the most approachable of men, relieved of every care and burden Perhaps, I thought—still trying to explain some oddness in her that I couldn't identify—she is the child of a daughter of his own who is dead.

"This is Mr. Zuckerman, the short-story writer," he said, teasing sweetly, like *my* grandfather now. "I gave you his collected works to read."

I rose and shook her hand.

"This is Miss Bellette. She was once a student here. She has been staying with us for a few days, and has taken it upon herself to begin sorting through my manuscripts. There is a movement afoot to persuade me to deposit with Harvard University the pieces of paper on which I turn my sentences around. Amy works for the Harvard library. The Athene library has just extended her an exceptional offer, but she tells us she is tied to her life in Cambridge. Meanwhile, she has cunningly been using the visit to try to persuade me—"

"No, no, no," she said emphatically. "If you see it that way, my cause is doomed." As if she hadn't charm enough, Miss Bellette's speech was made melodious by a faint foreign accent. "The maestro," she explained, turning my way, "is by temperament counter-suggestible."

"And counter that," he moaned, registering a mild protest against the psychological lingo.

"I've just found twenty-seven drafts of a single short story," she told me.

"Which story?" I asked eagerly.

"'Life Is Embarrassing.'"

"To get it wrong," said Lonoff, "so many times."

"They ought to construct a monument to your patience," she told him.

He gestured vaguely toward the crescent of plumpness buttoned in beneath his jacket. "They have."

"In class," she said, "he used to tell the writing students, 'There is no life without patience.' None of us knew what he was talking about."

"You knew. You had to know. My dear young lady, I learned that from watching you."

"But I can't wait for anything," she said.

"But you do."

"Bursting with frustration all the while."

"If you weren't bursting," her teacher informed her, "you wouldn't need patience."

At the hall closet she stepped out of the loafers she'd worn into the living room and slipped on white woolen socks and a pair of red snow boots. Then from a hanger she took down a plaid hooded jacket, into whose sleeve was tucked a white wool cap with a long tassel that ended in a fluffy white ball. Having seen her only seconds before banter so easily with the celebrated writer—having myself felt ever so slightly drawn into the inner circle by her easy, confident way with him—I was surprised by the childish hat. The costume, now that she had it on, seemed like a little girl's. That she could act so wise and dress up so young mystified me.

Along with Lonoff I stood in the open doorway waving goodbye. I was now in awe of two people in this house.

There was still more wind than snow, but in Lonoff's orchard the light had all but seeped away, and the sound of what was on

its way was menacing. Two dozen wild old
apple trees stood as first barrier between the
bleak unpaved road and the farmhouse. Next
came a thick green growth of rhododendron,
then a wide stone wall fallen in like a worn
molar at the center, then some fifty feet of
snow-crusted lawn, and finally, drawn up
close to the house and protectively overhang-
ing the shingles, three maples that looked
from their size to be as old as New England.
In back, the house gave way to unprotected
fields, drifted over since the first December
blizzards. From there the wooded hills began
their impressive rise, undulating forest swells
that just kept climbing into the next state.
My guess was that it would take even the
fiercest Hun the better part of a winter to
cross the glacial waterfalls and wind-blasted
woods of those mountain wilds before he was
able to reach the open edge of Lonoff's hay-
fields, rush the rear storm door of the house,
crash through into the study, and, with
spiked bludgeon wheeling high in the air
above the little Olivetti, cry out in a roaring
voice to the writer tapping out his twenty-
seventh draft, "You must change your life!"
And even he might lose heart and turn back
to the bosom of his barbarian family should
he approach those black Massachusetts hills

on a night like this, with the cocktail hour at hand and yet another snowstorm arriving from Ultima Thule. No, for the moment, at least, Lonoff seemed really to have nothing to worry about from the outside world.

We watched from the front step until Lonoff was sure that she had cleared both the windshield and rear window; snow had already begun adhering to the icy glass. "Drive very slowly," he called. To get into the diminutive green Renault she had to hike up a handful of long skirt. Above the snow boots I saw an inch of flesh, and quickly looked elsewhere so as not to be found out.

"Yes, be careful," I called to her, in the guise of Mr. Zuckerman the short-story writer. "It's slippery, it's deceptive."

"She has a remarkable prose style," Lonoff said to me when we were back inside the house. "The best student writing I've ever read. Wonderful clarity. Wonderful comedy. Tremendous intelligence. She wrote stories about the college which capture the place in a sentence. Everything she sees, she takes hold of. And a lovely pianist. She can play Chopin with great charm. She used to practice on our daughter's piano when she first came to Athene. That was something I looked forward to at the end of the day."

"She seems to be quite a girl," I said thoughtfully. "Where is she from originally?"

"She came to us from England."

"But the accent...?"

"That," he allowed, "is from the country of Fetching."

"I agree," I dared to say, and thought: Enough shyness then, enough boyish uncertainty and tongue-tied deference. This, after all, is the author of "Life Is Embarrassing"—if he doesn't know the score, who does?

Standing by the fire, the two of us warming ourselves, I turned to Lonoff and said, "I don't think I could keep my wits about me, teaching at a school with such beautiful and gifted and fetching girls."

To which he replied flatly, "Then you shouldn't do it."

A surprise—yes, yet another—awaited me when we sat down to dinner. Lonoff uncorked a bottle of Chianti that had been waiting for us on the table and proposed a toast. Signaling his wife to raise her glass along with his, he said, "To a wonderful new writer."

Well, *that* loosened me up. Excitedly, I began talking about my month at Quahsay,

how much I loved the serenity and beauty of
the place, how I loved walking the trails there
at the end of the day and reading in my room
at night—rereading Lonoff of late, but that
I kept to myself. From his toast it was obvious
that I had not lost as much ground as I feared
by confessing to the lure of clever, pretty college girls, and I did not want to risk offending
him anew by seeming to fawn. The fawning,
supersensitive Willis, I remembered, had
been given less than sixty seconds on the
phone.

I told the Lonoffs about the joy of awakening each morning knowing there were all
those empty hours ahead to be filled only with
work. Never as a student or a soldier or a
door-to-door salesman did I have regular
stretches of uninterrupted time to devote to
writing, nor had I ever lived before in such
quiet and seclusion, or with my few basic
needs so unobtrusively satisfied as they were
by the Quahsay housekeeping staff. It all
seemed to me a marvelous, a miraculous gift.
Just a few evenings before, after a day-long
snowstorm, I had accompanied the Colony
handyman when he set out after dinner on
the snowplow to clear the trails that twisted
for miles through the Quahsay woods. I described for the Lonoffs my exhilaration at

watching the snow crest in the headlights of the truck and then fall away into the forest; the bite of the cold and the smack of the tire chains had seemed to me all I could ever want at the end of a long day at *my* Olivetti. I supposed I was being professionally innocent despite myself, but I couldn't stop going on about my hours on the snowplow after the hours at my desk: it wasn't just that I wanted to convince Lonoff of my pure and incorruptible spirit—my problem was that I wanted to believe it myself. My problem was that I wanted to be wholly worthy of his thrilling toast. "I could live like that forever," I announced.

"Don't try it," he said. "If your life consists of reading and writing and looking at the snow, you'll wind up like me. Fantasy for thirty years."

Lonoff made "Fantasy" sound like a breakfast cereal.

Here for the first time his wife spoke up—though given the self-effacing delivery, "spoke down" would be more exact. She was a smallish woman with gentle gray eyes and soft white hair and a multitude of fine lines crisscrossing her pale skin. Though she could well have been, as the amused literati had it, Lonoff's "high-born Yankee heiress"—and an excellent example of the species at its most maidenly—what she looked like now was some frontier survivor, the wife of a New England farmer who long ago rode out of these mountains to make a new start in the West. To me the lined face and the shadowy, timorous manner bore witness to a grinding history of agonized childbearing and escapes from the Indians, of famine and fevers and wagon-train austerities—I just couldn't believe that she could look so worn down from living alongside E. I. Lonoff while he wrote short stories for thirty years. I was to learn later that aside from two terms at a Boston art school and a few months in New York— and the year in London trying to get Lonoff to Westminster Abbey—Hope had strayed no farther than had the locally prominent lawyers and clergymen who were her forebears, and whose legacy by now came to nothing more tangible than one of the Berkshires' "best" names and the house that went with it.

She had met Lonoff when he came at the age of seventeen to work for a chicken farmer in Lenox. He himself had been raised just outside Boston, though until he was five lived in Russia. After his father, a jeweler, nearly died from injuries suffered in the Zhitomir pogrom, Lonoff's parents emigrated to primitive Palestine. There typhus carried them both away, and their son was cared for by family friends in a Jewish farming settlement. At seven he was shipped alone from Jaffa to wealthy relatives of his father's in Brookline; at seventeen he chose vagabondage over college at the relatives' expense; and then at twenty he chose Hope—the rootless Levantine Valentino taking as his mate a cultivated young provincial woman, bound to the finer things by breeding and temperament, and to a settled place by old granite gravestones, church-meetinghouse plaques, and a long mountain road bearing the name Whittlesey: somebody from somewhere, for all the good that was to do him.

Despite everything that gave Hope Lonoff the obedient air of an aging geisha when she dared to speak or to move, I still wondered if she was not going to remind him that his life had consisted of something more than reading and writing and looking at snow: it had also consisted of her and the children. But there was not the hint of a reprimand in her unchallenging voice when she said, "You shouldn't express such a low opinion of your achievement. It's not becoming." Even more delicately, she added, "And it's not true."

44

Lonoff lifted his chin. "I was not measuring my achievement. I have neither too high nor too low an estimate of my work. I believe I know exactly wherein my value and originality lie. I know where I can go and just how far, without making a mockery of the thing we all love. I was only suggesting—surmising is more like it—that an unruly personal life will probably better serve a writer like Nathan than walking in the woods and startling the deer. His work has turbulence—that should be nourished, and not in the woods. All I was trying to say is that he oughtn't to stifle what is clearly his gift."

"I'm sorry," replied his wife. "I didn't understand. I thought you were expressing distaste for your own work." "Work" she pronounced in the accent of her region, without the "r."

"I was expressing distaste," said Lonoff, employing that pedantic tone he'd taken with Amy on the subject of her patience, and with me, describing his light-reading problem, "but not for the work. I was expressing distaste for the range of my imagination."

With a self-effacing smile designed to atone on the spot for her audacity, Hope said, "Your imagination or your experience?"

"I long ago gave up illusions about myself and experience."

She pretended to be brushing the crumbs from around the bread board, that and no more—while with unforeseen, somewhat inexplicable insistence, she softly confessed, "I never quite know what that means"

"It means I know who I am I know the kind of man I am and the kind of writer I have my own kind of bravery, and please, let's leave it at that."

She decided to. I remembered my food and began to eat again.

"Do you have a girl friend?" Lonoff asked me.

I explained the situation—to the extent that I was willing to.

Betsy had found out about me and a girl she had known since ballet school. The two of us had kissed over a glass of Gallo in the kitchen, playfully she had shown me the tip of her wine-stained tongue, and I, quick to take heart, had pulled her out of her chair and down beside the sink. This took place one evening when Betsy was off dancing at the City Center and the friend had stopped by to pick up a record and investigate a flirtation we'd begun some months earlier, when Betsy was away touring with the company. On my

46

knees, I struggled to unclothe her; not resisting all that strenuously, she, on her knees, told me what a bastard I was to be doing this to Betsy. I refrained from suggesting that she might be less than honorable herself; trading insults while in heat wasn't my brand of aphrodisia, and I was afraid of a fiasco if I should try it and get carried away. So, shouldering the burden of perfidy for two, I pinned her pelvis to the kitchen linoleum, while she continued, through moist smiling lips, to inform me of my character flaws. I was then at the stage of my erotic development when nothing excited *me* as much as having intercourse on the floor.

Betsy was a romantic, excitable, highstrung girl who could be left quivering by the backfire of a car—so when the friend intimated over the phone to her a few days later that I wasn't to be trusted, it nearly destroyed her. It was a bad time for her, anyway. Yet another of her rivals had been cast as a cygnet in *Swan Lake*, and so, four years after having been enlisted by Balanchine as a seventeen-year-old of great promise, she had yet to rise out of the corps and it didn't look to her now as though she ever would. And how she worked to be the best! Her art was everything, a point of view no less beguiling to me

than the large painted gypsy-girl eyes and
the small unpainted she-monkey face, and
those elegant, charming tableaux she could
achieve, even when engaged in something so
aesthetically unpromising as, half asleep in
the middle of the night, taking a lonely pee
in my bathroom. When we were first introduced in New York, I knew nothing about
ballet and had never seen a real dancer on
the stage, let alone off. An Army friend who'd
grown up next door to Betsy in Riverdale had
gotten us tickets for a Tchaikovsky extrava-
ganza and then arranged for a girl who was
dancing in it to have coffee with us around
the corner from the City Center that afternoon. Fresh from rehearsal and enchantingly
full of herself, Betsy amused us by recounting
the horrors of her self-sacrificing vocation—
a cross, as she described it, between the life
of a boxer and the life of a nun. And the worrying! She had begun studying at the age of
eight and had been worrying ever since about
her height and her weight and her ears and
her rivals and her injuries and her chances—
right now she was in absolute terror about
tonight. I myself couldn't see that she had
reason to be anxious about anything (least
of all those ears), so entranced was I already
by the dedication and the glamour. At the

theater I unfortunately couldn't remember—
once the music had begun and dozens of danc-
ers rushed on stage—whether earlier she
had told us that she was one of the girls in
lavender with a pink flower in their hair or
one of the girls in pink with a lavender flower
in their hair, and so I spent most of the evening just trying to find her. Each time I
thought that the legs and arms I was watching were Betsy's, I became so elated I wanted
to cheer—but then another pack of ten came
streaking across the stage and I thought, No,
there, *that's* her.

"You were wonderful," I told her afterward. "Yes? Did you like my little solo? It's
not actually a solo—it lasts only about fifteen
seconds. But I do think it's awfully charming." "Oh, I thought it was terrific," I said,
"it seemed like more than fifteen seconds to
me."

A year later our artistic and amatory al-
liance came to an end when I confessed that
the mutual friend had not been the first girl
to be dragged onto the floor while Betsy was
safely off dancing her heart out and I had
nighttime hours with nothing to do and nobody to stop me. I had been at this for some
time now and, I admitted, it was no way to
be treating her. Bold honesty, of course, pro-

49

duced far more terrible results than if I had only confessed to seducing the wily seductress and left it at that; nobody had asked me about anybody else. But carried away by the idea that if I were a perfidious brute, I at least would be a truthful perfidious brute, I was crueler than was either necessary or intended. In a fit of penitential gloom, I fled from New York to Quahsay, where eventually I managed to absolve myself of the sin of lust and the crime of betrayal by watching from behind the blade of the snowplow as it cleared the Colony roads for my solitary and euphoric walks—walks during which I did not hesitate to embrace trees and kneel down and kiss the glistening snow, so bursting was I with a sense of gratitude and freedom and renewal.

Of all this, I told the Lonoffs only the charming part about how we had met and also that now, sadly, my girl friend and I were trying a temporary separation. Otherwise, I portrayed her in such uxorious detail that, along with the unnerving sense that I might be laying it on a little thick for this old married couple, I wound up in wonder at the idiot I had been to relinquish her love. Describing all her sterling qualities, I had, in fact, brought myself nearly to the point of grief, as though instead of wailing with pain and telling me to leave and never come back, the unhappy dancer had died in my arms on our wedding day.

Hope Lonoff said, "I knew that she was a dancer from the *Saturday Review* "

The *Saturday Review* had published an article on America's young, unknown writers, photographs and thumbnail sketches of "A Dozen to Keep Your Eye On," selected by the editors of the major literary quarterlies I had been photographed playing with Nijinsky, our cat. I had confessed to the interviewer that my "friend" was with the New York City Ballet, and when asked to name the three living writers I admired most, I had listed E. I. Lonoff first.

I was disturbed now to think that this must have been the first Lonoff had heard of me—though, admittedly, while answering the interviewer's impossible questions, I had been hoping that my comment might bring my work to his attention. The morning the magazine appeared on the newsstands I must have read the bit about "N. Zuckerman" fifty times over. I tried to put in my self-prescribed six hours at the typewriter but got nowhere, what with picking up the article and looking at my picture every five minutes. I don't know

Philip Roth

what I expected to see revealed there—the future probably, the titles of my first ten books—but I do remember thinking that this photograph of an intense and serious young writer playing so gently with a kitty cat, and said to be living in a five-flight Village walk-up with a young ballerina, might inspire any number of thrilling women to want to try to take her place.

"I would never have allowed that to appear," I said, "if I had realized how it was all going to come out. They interviewed me for an hour and then what they used of what I said was nonsense."

"Don't apologize," said Lonoff.

"Don't indeed," said his wife, smiling at me. "What's wrong with having your picture in the paper?"

"I didn't mean the picture—though that, too. I never knew they were going to use the one of me with the cat. I expected they'd use the one at the typewriter. I should have realized they couldn't show everybody at a typewriter. The girl who came around to take the pictures"—and whom I had tried unsuccessfully to throw onto the floor—"said she'd just take the picture of the cat for Betsy and me."

"Don't apologize," Lonoff repeated, "unless you know for sure you're not going to do it again next time. Otherwise, just do it and forget it. Don't make a production out of it."

Hope said, "He only means he understands, Nathan. He has the highest respect for what you are. We don't have visitors unless they're people Manny respects. He has no tolerance for people without substance."

"Enough," said Lonoff.

"I just don't want Nathan to resent you for superiority feelings you don't have."

"My wife would have been happier with a less exacting companion."

"But you *are* less exacting," she said, "with everyone but yourself. Nathan, you don't have to defend yourself. Why shouldn't you enjoy your first bit of recognition? Who deserves it more than a gifted young man like yourself? Think of all the worthless people held up for our esteem every day: movie stars, politicians, athletes. Because you happen to be a writer doesn't mean you have to deny yourself the ordinary human pleasure of being praised and applauded."

"Ordinary human pleasures have nothing to do with it. Ordinary human pleasures be damned. The young man wants to be an artist."

"Sweetheart," she replied, "you must sound to Nathan so—so unyielding. And you're

really not that way at all. You're the most
forgiving and understanding and modest person I have ever known. Too modest."

"Let's forget how I sound and have dessert."

"But you are the kindest person. He is,
Nathan. You've met Amy, haven't you?"

"Miss Bellette?"

"Do you know all he's done for her? She
wrote him a letter when she was sixteen
years old. In care of his publisher. The most
charming, lively letter—so daring, so brash.
She told him her story, and instead of for-
getting it, he wrote her back. He has always
written people back—a polite note even to
the fools."

"What was her story?" I asked.

"Displaced," said Lonoff. "Refugee." That
seemed to him to suffice, though not to the
wagon-train wife, who surprised me now by
the way that she pressed on. Was it the little
bit of wine that had gone to her head? Or was
there not something seething in her?

"She said she was a highly intelligent, creative, and charming sixteen-year-old who
was now living with a not very intelligent,
creative, or charming family in Bristol, England. She even included her IQ," Hope said.
"No, no, that was the second letter. Anyway,

she said she wanted a new start in life and she thought the man whose wonderful story she'd read in her school anthology—"

"It wasn't an anthology, but you might as well keep going."

Hope tried her luck with a self-effacing smile, but the wattage was awfully dim. "I think I can talk about this without help. I'm only relating the facts, and calmly enough, I had thought. Because the story was in a magazine, and not in an anthology, doesn't mean that I have lost control of myself. Furthermore, Amy is not the subject, not by any means. The subject is your extraordinary kindness and charity. Your concern for anyone in need—anyone except yourself, and your needs."

"Only my 'self,' as you like to call it, happens not to exist in the everyday sense of the word. Consequently, you may stop lavishing praise upon it. And worrying about its 'needs.'"

"But your self *does* exist. It has a perfect *right* to exist—and in the everyday sense!"

"Enough," he suggested again.

With that, she rose to begin to clear the dishes for dessert, and all at once a wineglass struck the wall. Hope had thrown it. "Chuck me out," she cried, "I want you to chuck me out. Don't tell me you can't, because you must! I want you to! I'll finish the dishes, then chuck me out, tonight! I beg of you—I'd rather live and die alone, I'd rather endure that than another moment of your bravery! I cannot take any more moral fiber in the face of life's disappointments! Not yours and not mine! I cannot bear having a loyal, dignified husband who has no illusions about himself *one second more!*"

My heart, of course, was pounding away, though not entirely because the sound of glass breaking and the sight of a disappointed woman, miserably weeping, was new to me. It was about a month old. On our last morning together Betsy had broken every dish of the pretty little Bloomingdale's set that we owned in common, and then, while I hesitated about leaving my apartment without making my position clear, she started in on the glassware. The hatred for me I had inspired by telling the whole truth had me particularly confused. If only I had lied, I thought—if only I had said that the friend who had intimated I might not be trustworthy was a troublemaking bitch, jealous of Betsy's success and not a little crazy, none of this would be happening. But then, if I had lied to her, I would have *lied* to her. Except that what I would have said about the friend would in essence have been true! I didn't get it. Nor did Betsy when I tried to calm her down and explain what a swell fellow I actually was to have been so candid about it all. It was here, in fact, that she set about destroying the slender drinking glasses, a set of six from Sweden that we had bought to replace the jelly jars on a joyous quasi-connubial outing some months earlier at Bonniers (bought along with the handsome Scandinavian throw rug onto which, in due course, I had tried to drag the photographer from the *Saturday Review*).

Hope Lonoff had now slumped back into her chair, the better to plead with her husband across the table. Her face was patched with blotches where she had been digging at the soft, creased skin in a fit of self-abasement. The frantic, agitated movement of her fingers alarmed me more even than the misery in her voice, and I wondered if I shouldn't reach over and pick up the serving fork from the table before she turned the prongs into her bosom and gave Lonoff's "self" the freedom to pursue what she thought it needed. But as I was only a guest—as I was "only" just about anything you could think of—I left all cutlery where it was and waited for the worst.

"Take her, Manny. If you want her, take

her," she cried, "and then you won't be so
miserable, and everything in the world won't
be so bleak. She's not a student any more—
she's a woman! You are *entitled* to her—you
rescued her from oblivion, you are more than
entitled: it's the only thing that makes sense!
Tell her to accept that job, tell her to stay!
She should! And I'll move away! Because I
cannot live another moment as your jailer!
Your nobility is eating away the last thing
that is left! You are a monument and can
take it and take it—but I'm down to nothing,
darling, and I can't. Chuck me out! Please,
now, before your goodness and your wisdom
kill us both!"

Lonoff and I sat talking together in the living
room after dinner, each sipping with admirable temperance at the tablespoonful of cognac he had divided between two large snif-
ters. I had so far experienced brandy only as
a stopgap household remedy for toothache: a
piece of absorbent cotton, soaked in the stuff,
would be pressed against my throbbing gum
until my parents could get me to the dentist.
I accepted Lonoff's offer, however, as though
it accorded with my oldest post-prandial cus-
tom. The comedy thickened when my host,
another big drinker, went to look for the right

glasses. After a systematic search he finally found them at the rear of the bottom cabinet in the foyer breakfront. "A gift," he explained, "I thought they were still in the box," and took two into the kitchen to wash away dust that seemed to have been accumulating since the time of Napoleon, whose name was on the sealed brandy bottle. While he was at it he decided to wash the four other glasses in the set, and put them back in hiding in the breakfront before rejoining me to begin our merrymaking at the hearth.

Not much later—in all, maybe twenty minutes after he had refused to respond in any way to her plea to be replaced by Amy Bellette—Hope could be heard in the kitchen, washing the dishes that Lonoff and I had silently cleared from the table following her departure. She seemed to have gotten down from their bedroom by a back stairway— probably so as not to disturb our conversation.

While helping him to clear up, I had not known what to do about her broken wineglass or about the saucer she inadvertently had knocked to the floor when she rushed from the table. My duty as ingenue was clearly to spare the stout man in the business suit from bending over, especially as he was E. I. Lonoff; on the other hand, I was still trying to get through by pretending that nothing shocking had happened in my presence. To keep the tantrum in perspective, he might even prefer that the broken bits be left where they were for Hope to clean up later, provided she did not first commit suicide in their room.

Even as my sense of moral niceties and my youthful cowardice battled it out with my naïveté, Lonoff, groaning slightly from the effort, brushed the glass into a dustpan and retrieved the saucer from beneath the dining table. It had broken neatly in two, and after inspecting the edges he observed, "She can glue it."

In the kitchen he left the dish for her to repair on a long wooden counter where pink and white geraniums were growing in clay pots beneath the windows. The kitchen was a bright, pretty room a little cheerier and livelier looking than the rest of the house. Besides the geraniums flowering abundantly here even in winter, tall reeds and dried flowers were stuck all about in pitchers and vases and little odd-shaped bottles. The windowed wall cupboards were bright and homey and reassuring: food staples labeled with unimpeachable brand names—enough Bumble Bee tuna for an Eskimo family to survive on in their igloo till spring—and jars of tomatoes, beans, pears, crabapples, and the like, which seemed to have been put up by Hope herself. Pots and pans with shining copper bottoms hung in rows from a pegboard beside the stove, and along the wall above the breakfast table were half a dozen pictures in plain wooden frames, which turned out to be short nature poems signed "H.L.," copied in delicate calligraphy and decorated with watercolor designs. It did indeed look to be the headquarters of a woman who, in her own unostentatious way, could glue anything and do anything, except figure out how to make her husband happy.

We talked about literature and I was in heaven—also in a sweat from the spotlight he was giving me to bask in. Every book new to me I was sure he must have annotated with his reading pen long ago, yet his interest was pointedly in hearing my thoughts, not his own. The effect of his concentrated attention was to make me heap insight onto precocious insight, and then to hang upon his every sigh and grimace, investing what was only a little bout of after-dinner dyspepsia with the direst implications about my taste and my intelligence. Though I worried that I was trying too hard to sound like the kind of deep thinker for whom he had no love, I still couldn't stop myself, under the spell now not just of the man and his accomplishment but of the warm wood fire, of the brandy snifter balanced in my hand (if not yet the brandy), and of the snow falling heavily beyond the cushioned windowseats, as dependably beautiful and mystifying as ever Then there were the great novelists, whose spellbinding names I chanted as I laid my cross-cultural comparisons and brand-new eclectic enthusiasms at his fee Zuckerman, with Lonoff, discussing Kafka. I couldn't quite get it, let alone get over it. And then there was his dinner-table toast. It still gave me a temperature of a hundred and five each time I remembered it. To myself I swore that I would struggle for the rest of my life to deserve it. And wasn't that why he'd proposed it, this pitiless new master of mine?

"I've just finished reading Isaac Babel," I told him.

He considered this, impassively.

"I was thinking, for sport more or less, that he is the missing link; those stories are what connect you, if you don't mind my mentioning your work—"

He crossed his hands on his belly and rested them there, movement enough to make me say, "I'm sorry."

"Go ahead. Connected to Babel. How?"

"Well, 'connected' of course isn't the right word. Neither is 'influence.' It's family resemblance that I'm talking about. It's as though, as I see it, you are Babel's American cousin—and Felix Abravanel is the other. You through 'The Sin of Jesus' and something in *Red Cavalry*, through the ironical dreaming and the blunt reporting, and, of course, through the writing itself. Do you see what I mean? There's a sentence in one of his war stories: 'Voroshilov combed his horse's mane with his Mauser.' Well, that's just the kind of thing that you do, a stunning little picture in every line. Babel said that if he ever wrote his autobiography he'd call it *The Story of an Adjective*. Well, if it were possible to imagine you writing your autobiography—if such a thing were even imaginable—you might come up with that title too. No?"

"And Abravanel?"

"Oh, with Abravanel it's Benya Krik and the Odessa mob: the gloating, the gangsters, all those gigantic types. It isn't that he throws in his sympathy with the brutes—it isn't that in Babel, either. It's their awe of them. Even when they're appalled, they're in awe. Deep reflective Jews a little lovesick at the sound of all that un-Talmudic bone

63

crunching. Sensitive Jewish sages, as Babel says, dying to climb trees."

"'In my childhood I led the life of a sage, when I grew up I started climbing trees.'"

"Yes, that's the line," said I, expecting no less but still impressed. On I went. "Look at Abravanel's *Properly Scalded*. Movie moguls, union moguls, racketeer moguls, women who are moguls just with their breasts—even the down and out bums who used to be moguls, talking like moguls of the down and out. It's Babel's fascination with big-time Jews, with conscienceless Cossacks, with everybody who has it his own way. The Will as the Big Idea. Except Babel doesn't come off so lovable and enormous himself. That's not how he sees things. He is a sort of Abravanel with the self-absorption drained away. And if you drain away enough, well, in the end you arrive at Lonoff."

"And what about you?"

"Me?"

"Yes. You haven't finished. Aren't you a New World cousin in the Babel clan, too? What is Zuckerman in all of this?"

"Why—nothing. I've only published the four stories that I sent you. My relationship is nonexistent. I think I'm still at the point where my relationship to my *own* work is practically nonexistent."

So I said, and quickly reached for my glass so as to duck my disingenuous face and take a bitter drop of brandy on my tongue. But Lonoff had read my designing mind, all right; for when I came upon Babel's description of the Jewish writer as a man with autumn in his heart and spectacles on his nose, I had been inspired to add, "and blood in his penis," and had then recorded the words like a challenge—a flaming Dedalian formula to ignite *my* soul's smithy.

"What else?" Lonoff asked. "Come on, don't get bashful. This is enjoyable. Talk, please."

"About—?"

"All these books you read."

"Your books included or excluded?" I asked him.

"Suit yourself."

I said, "I think of you as the Jew who got away."

"And does that help?"

"There's *some* truth in it, isn't there? You got away from Russia and the pogroms. You got away from the purges—and Babel didn't. You got away from Palestine and the homeland. You got away from Brookline and the relatives. You got away from New York—"

"And all of this is recorded where? Hedda Hopper?"

"Some there. The rest I pieced together myself."

"To what end?"

"When you admire a writer you become curious. You look for his secret. The clues to his puzzle."

"But New York—I was there for three months over twenty years ago. Who told you I got away from New York?"

"Some of the Jews down there you got away from."

"I was there for three months and I think I got a word in only once. What word I don't remember, but suddenly I belonged to a faction."

"That's why you left?"

"Also, there was the girl I'd fallen in love with and married. She wasn't happy."

"Why not?"

"Same as me. Those were terrifying intellectual personalities even back then. Real ideological Benya Kriks, even in their diapers. I didn't have enough strong opinions to last me down there through a year. My Hope had even fewer."

"So you came back here, you got away for good."

"From Jews? Not altogether. The game warden tells me there are some more up in these woods besides me. But you're more or less right. It's the deer in their fields that drive the farmers crazy, not the few of us they see around here in caftans. But where's the secret, Nathan? What's the puzzle?"

"Away from all the Jews, and a story by you without a Jew in it is unthinkable. The deer, the farmers, the game warden—"

"And don't forget Hope. And my fair-haired children."

"And still all you write about are Jews."

"Proving what?"

"That," I said, cautiously, "is what I'd like to ask you."

He thought about it for a moment. "It proves why the young rabbi in Pittsfield can't live with the idea that I won't be 'active.'"

I waited for more, but in vain.

"Do you know Abravanel?" I asked.

"Nathan, surely by now you get the picture."

"What picture?"

"I don't know anybody. I turn sentences around, and that's it. Why would Abravanel want to know me? I put him to sleep. He spoke at Amherst last spring. An invitation arrived so we drove over to hear him. But that's the only time we've ever met. Before the lecture he came down the aisle to where I was sitting and introduced himself. He was very flattering. My respectful younger colleague. Afterward we had a drink with him and his actress. A very polished fellow. The satirist you don't really see till you catch the commedia dell'arte profile. There's where the derision lives. Head-on he's something of a heartthrob. Bombay black eyes, and so on. And the young Israeli wife is like lava. The Gentile dream of the melon-breasted Jewess. And the black head of coarse curly hair—the long female version of his. You could polish a pot with it. They tell me that when she played in the big movie of the Bible she stole the show from the Creation. So there were those two, and there was I with Hope. And with this," he said, once more lightly laying his hands on his belly. "I understand he does a humorous imitation of me for his friends. No harm intended. One of my former students ran into him in Paris. He'd just addressed a full house at the Sorbonne. I'm told that upon hearing my name he referred to me as 'the complete man—as unimpressive as he is unimpressed.'"

"You don't like him much."

"I'm not in the business. 'Liking people' is often just another racket. But you're right to think well of his books. Not up my alley maybe, all that vanity face to face, but when he writes he's not just a little Houyhnhnm tapping out his superiority with his hooves. More like a Dr. Johnson eating opium—the disease of his life makes Abravanel fly. I admire the man, actually. I admire what he puts his nervous system through. I admire his passion for the front-row seat. Beautiful wives, beautiful mistresses, alimony the size of the national debt, polar expeditions, warfront reportage, famous friends, famous enemies, breakdowns, public lectures, five-hundred-page novels every third year, and still, as you said before, time and energy left over for all that self-absorption. The gigantic types in the books *have* to be that big to give him something to think about to rival himself. Like him? No. But impressed, oh yes. Absolutely. It's no picnic up there in the egosphere. I don't know when the man sleeps, or if he has ever slept, aside from those few minutes when he had that drink with me."

Outside, it was like a silent-film studio, where they made snowstorms by hurling mattress wadding into a wind machine. Large, ragged snowclots raced across the window, and when I heard their icy edges nicking at the glass—and the sounds of someone puttering in the kitchen—I remembered Lonoff's wife begging to be discarded, and wondered if the plea would have been quite so thoroughgoing on a sunny spring day. "I think I better get the taxi," I said, pointing to my watch, "so as to catch the last bus back."

Of course, I wanted never to leave. True, while Hope was falling apart at the dinner table I had momentarily found myself wishing for my cabin at Quahsay; now, however, the way the crisis seemed magically to have resolved itself served only to intensify my awe of Lonoff, particularly for what he unblushingly had called *my own kind of bravery*. If only I had thought to take his approach when Betsy had gone wild; if only I had kept my mouth shut until she finished berating me, then swept up the broken crockery and settled into my chair to read another book! Now, why didn't I? Because I was twenty-three and he was fifty-six? Or because I was guilty and he was innocent? Yes, his authority, and the rapid restoration of household sanity and order, might well owe something to that. "Take her! It's the only thing that makes sense!" cried Hope, and Lonoff's easy victory seemed to reside in never even having wanted to.

I also hated calling a taxi because of Amy Bellette. I was hoping, a little crazily, that when she came back from dinner with the college librarian, she would offer to drive me through the storm to my bus. Earlier, while Lonoff was measuring out the brandy—concentrating like a bartender who'd trained at Los Alamos with fissionable fifths—I had asked where she went. I hadn't the nerve to inquire about her status as a displaced person. But at the table, when he'd said that she had come to Athene as a refugee, I was reminded of "the children starving in Europe" whom we had heard so much about when we were children eating in New Jersey. If Amy had been one of them, perhaps that explained the something in her that seemed to me thwarted and underdeveloped, despite the dazzling maturity and severe good looks. I wondered if the dark refugee girl with the curious name Bellette could be Jewish, and in Europe had suffered from worse than starvation.

"Yes," said Lonoff, "you'd better call the taxi."

Reluctantly I stood to go.

"Or, if you like," he said, "you can stay over and sleep in the study."

"No, I think I really have to be off," I said, and cursed the upbringing that had taught me never to be greedy about second helpings. How much better if I had been raised in the gutter! Only how would I have gotten from the gutter to here?

"Suit yourself," Lonoff told me.

"I wouldn't want to inconvenience your wife."

"I think it will disturb her more if you leave than if you stay. She might hold herself responsible. I'm certain she would."

I pretended I had taken my dinner on the moon. "But why?"

"Sit down. Stay for breakfast, Nathan."

"I'd better not. I shouldn't."

"You know who Jimmy Durante is?"

"Of course."

"Do you know the old Durante number 'Did you ever have the feeling that you wanted to go, still have the feeling that you wanted to stay'?"

"Yes."

"Sit."

I sat—suiting myself, as the man said.

"Besides," he told me, "if you go now, you'll leave most of your cognac."

"If I go, so will you."

"Well, the Jew who got away didn't get away altogether." He smiled at me. "You don't have to finish it, just because you're staying. That's not part of the deal."

"No, no, I want to," I said, and took my biggest sip of the night. Saluting me with his glass, he followed suit.

"Hope will be pleased," he said. "She misses people. She misses the children and their friends. She went to art school in Boston before I brought her back here, sixteen versts to the nearest railway station. Manhattan terrified her, but Boston's her Moscow, she'd move there tomorrow. She thinks I would enjoy it in Cambridge. But all I need are those dinner parties. I'd rather talk to the horse."

"You have a horse?"

"No."

I loved him! Yes, nothing less than love for this man with no illusions: love for the bluntness, the scrupulosity, the severity, the estrangement; love for the relentless winnowing out of the babyish, preening, insatiable self; love for the artistic mulishness and the

73

suspicion of nearly everything else; and love for the buried charm, of which he'd just given me a glimpse. Yes, all Lonoff had to say was that he did not even have the horse to talk to and somehow that did it, released in me a son's girlish love for the man of splendid virtue and high achievement who understands life, and who understands the son, and who approves.

I should mention here that some three years earlier, after several hours in the presence of Felix Abravanel, I had been no less overcome. But if I did not fall at his feet straightaway, it was because even a college senior as writer-worshipping as myself could see that with Abravanel such boundless adoration—at least if offered up by a youthful male admirer—was doomed to go unrequited. The ardor of those books, composed in the sunny stillness of his California canyon and seething with unbuttoned and aggressive innocence, seemed to have little to do with the author himself when he came coolly out into the fallen world he'd been so ardent about down in the canyon. In fact, the writer who found irresistible all vital and dubious types, not excluding the swindlers of both sexes who trampled upon the large hearts of his optimistic, undone heroes; the writer who could locate the hypnotic core in the most devious American self-seeker and lead him to disclose, in spirited locutions all his own, the depths of his conniving soul; the writer whose absorption with "the grand human discord" made his every paragraph a little novel in itself, every page packed as tight as Dickens or Dostoevsky with the latest news of manias, temptations, passions, and dreams, with mankind aflame with feeling—well, in the flesh he gave the impression of being out to lunch.

Which isn't to suggest that Felix Abravanel lacked charm. On the contrary, the charm was like a moat so oceanic that you could not even see the great turreted and buttressed thing it had been dug to protect. You couldn't even find the drawbridge. He was like California itself—to get there you had to take a plane. There were moments during his public lecture—this was at Chicago, my last year there—when Abravanel had to pause at the lectern, seemingly to suppress saying something off the cuff that would have been just too charming for his audience to bear. And he was right. We might have charged the stage to eat him up alive if he had been any more sly and enchanting and wise. Poor marvelous Abravanel (I mean this without satire)—even what was intended to guard the great rose window of his inner brilliance was itself so damn beautiful that the ungifted multitudes and art lovers of the world could not but find him all the more alluring. On the other hand, maybe he wanted it that way. There is obviously no simple way to be great, or so I was beginning to find out.

After the lecture I had been invited to come along to a faculty-club reception by the professor whose protégé I was. When we were able at last to break through the rings of admirers, I was introduced as the student whose story would be discussed the next morning in the class Abravanel had consented to visit. From the dash of imperiousness in the photographed face I had never envisioned him quite so guarded-looking, or with a head a good size and a half too small for the six-foot plank that supported it. He reminded me, amid all those who would flatter and adore him, of a radio tower with its tiny red light burning high up to warn off low-flying aircraft. He wore a five-hundred-dollar shantung suit, a burgundy silk tie, and gleaming narrow black tasseled loafers, but everything that counted, all that made for the charm and the laughs and the books and the breakdowns, was stored compactly right up there at the top—at the edge of a precipice. It was a head that the Japanese technicians, with their ingenuity for miniaturizing, might have designed, and then given over to the Jews to adorn with the rug dealer's thinning dark hair, the guarded appraising black eyes, and a tropical bird's curving bill. A fully Semiticized little transistor on top, terrific clothes down below—and still the overall impression was of somebody's stand-in.

I thought, In the novels nothing ever seems to get by him, so how come when he's here, he's not? Perhaps so much assails him that he has to close down ninety percent of himself to phenomena in order not to explode. Though then again, I thought, maybe he's just out to lunch.

Abravanel shook my hand obligingly and was about to turn away to shake another obligingly when the professor repeated my name. "Of course," said Abravanel, "N. Zuckerman." He had read a mimeographed copy of my story on the plane from the Coast; so had Andrea read it. "Sweetheart," he said, "this is Zuckerman."

Well, where to begin? Andrea had maybe only five years on me, but five years put to good use. After graduating from Sarah Lawrence, she had evidently continued her edu-

cation at Elizabeth Arden and Henri Bendel.
As we all knew—her fame having preceded
her—Andrea's father had been a dollar-a-
year man in the first Roosevelt Administra-
tion, and Mother was Carla Peterson Rumbough, the loquacious liberal congresswoman
from Oregon. While still a college student she
had written the first of her portraits of "Men
in Power" for *The Saturday Evening Post*, the
series eventually collected in her best-selling
book. Undoubtedly (as the envious were
quick enough to point out), family contacts
had got her going, but clearly what encour-
aged those busy and powerful men to keep on
talking was the proximity of Andrea herself,
for Andrea was a most juicy girl. Truly, you
felt that if you pressed her, you could drink
a glassful of refreshing, healthy Andrea for
breakfast.

At the time, she was in residence with
Abravanel at his Pacific Palisades retreat, a
few miles from the home of his friend and
mentor, Thomas Mann. ("The grand human
discord" was how Mann had perceived Abravanel's subject in the elevating preface with
which he had consecrated the German edition
of *Properly Scalded*.) After Abravanel's latest
divorce (and rumored emotional collapse),
Andrea had come to interview him for the

Post series and, as transcontinental literary
legend had it, had never left. Legend also had
it that Abravanel was not only the first man
of letters to be named a man of power in
America but the first man of power to whose
advances Andrea had yielded. I myself wondered if maybe Andrea wasn't the first journalist to whose advances Abravanel had
yielded. He looked more like the one who
would have had to be seduced.

"How terrific finally to meet you," Andrea
said, briskly shaking my hand. The briskness
of the handshake was in disarming contrast
with the soft voluptuous appearance. The
face was heart-shaped and gentle, but the
handshake said, "Have no doubts, I am the
girl who has everything." Not that I was
about to argue. I was already convinced a
month before laying eyes on her, when we
had exchanged letters about hotel accom-
modations. As student representative of the
University Lecture Committee, I had, per her
instructions, reserved a room in their two
names at the Windermere, the closest the
neighborhood had to a grand hotel. "Mr.
Abravanel and Miss Rumbough?" the desk
clerk had asked. "Are they husband and wife,
sir?" This question was put to me, mind you,
in March of 1953, and so when I answered

with the lie that I had devised to shelter a hero from scandal—"Mrs. Abravanel is the well-known journalist; that of course is her professional name"—I was sure that the end result of Miss A. Rumbough's bohemian daring would be my expulsion from college without a degree.

"I loved your story," she said. "It's *so* funny."

Grimly I acknowledged the compliment tendered my wit by the bosomy girl with the heart-shaped face and the milkmaid complexion and the soldierly self-assured grip. In the meantime, having passed me on to Andrea to dispose of, Abravanel found himself being exhibited by another of our professors to a huddle of graduate students waiting shyly beside their teacher to ask the writer serious questions. "Oh, well," I heard him say, with a light annihilating laugh, "I don't have the time these days to think about 'influences'—Andrea keeps me pretty much on the run." "Felix," she was telling me, "is nuts about the story, too. You should have seen him on the plane. He just kept throwing back his head and laughing. Where are you going to publish it? Maybe Felix ought to talk to—" She mentioned a name. It was Knebel, but for one whose stories had appeared previously only in the college literary quarterly, the effect would have been no more stunning if she had said, "After the reception I have to get back to the hotel to interview Marshal Tito in the bar—but while I do, Felix can rise unto Heaven from the lobby and discuss your funny little mimeographed story with the author of *The Brothers Karamazov*. We all met in Siberia when Felix and I did the prison tour." Somewhere behind me I heard Abravanel applying himself to another serious question from the graduate division. "Alienation? Oh," he said, with that light laugh, "let the other guy be alienated." Simultaneously Andrea informed me, "He's seeing Sy tomorrow night in New York—" (Sy being Knebel, the editor for twenty years of the New York intellectual quarterly that I had been devouring for the past two).

The next day Abravanel visited our advanced-writing class, accompanied—to the surprise of those ready to live only for art— by the bold Andrea. Her luminous, shameless presence in the very front row (and her white jersey dress; and her golden hair, out of some rustic paradise) led me to recall October afternoons half a lifetime ago when I sat like a seething prisoner, practicing my penmanship at my sloping school desk while the

World Series was being broadcast live to dinky radios in every gas station in America. It was then that I learned what tore at the hearts of the delinquents and the dummies who loathed the classroom and the teacher and wished the whole place would burn down.

Hands plunged into his pockets, and angled casually against the professor's desk, Abravanel spoke of my story with oblique admiration, defending it, largely with his laugh, from criticism brought by the orthodox Forsterites that my narrator was "two-dimensional" instead of being "round" like the characters they'd read about in *Aspects of the Novel*. But that day to all carping I was immune. *Andrea*, I thought, whenever one of those fools said "round."

Afterward I was invited by Abravanel for a cup of coffee at a local luncheonette, along with Andrea, my professor, and a member of the sociology department, an old friend from Abravanel's youth who had been waiting outside the classroom door to give Abravanel a nostalgic hug (which the author managed graciously to accept even while backing away). Abravanel had extended the invitation personally (as I was to write my parents) and with what sounded for the first time like real sympathy: "They're a rough bunch, Zuckerman. You better come along for a transfusion." I figured he would tell me over the cup of coffee that he was taking his copy of my story to New York to show to Seymour Knebel. For a hundred reasons I was in ecstasy. When he told me to come along for my transfusion, I could not remember having *myself* ever felt like such a round character before. What Mann had done for him he was about to do for me. Literary history in the making. Good thing Andrea was there to get it all down for posterity.

But over his coffee Abravanel said not a word: just leaned his long demi-emaciated frame back in his chair, looking smooth and strokable as a cat in his teaching attire of soft gray flannel slacks, a light mauve pullover, and a cashmere sports coat. With hands and ankles elegantly crossed, he left it to his buoyant young companion to do the talking— lively, funny stories, mostly, about Felix's old father, an L.A. housepainter, and the winning remarks he made to her in his homely mix of two languages. Even the sociology professor was bowled over, though from campus gossip I knew he was a dear friend of Abravanel's litigious first wife and disapproved of the writer's treatment of her, first in the flesh, then in fiction. Moreover, he was said to disapprove of Abravanel's way with women generally and, on top of that, believed that a novelist of his stature oughtn't to have articles about himself in *The Saturday Evening Post*. Yet now the sociology professor began lifting his voice so as to get Andrea to hear him. As a boy, he also had been a great fan of Felix's father's malapropisms, and he wanted it known. "'That fellow,'" shouted the sociologist, imitating the elder Abravanel, "'he ain't here no more—poor guy committed suitcase.'" If Abravanel thought the retired housepainter was so impressive for speaking cockeyed English all his life, he didn't let on. So genteel and assured and courtly was the posture he'd assumed to listen to Andrea tell her stories that I found myself doubting it. Out in the open, Abravanel's cup did not spill over with sentiment for the old days in L.A.; such effusions he left to readers of his novels who had come to love the super-charged emotional world of his childhood as though it had been their own. He himself seemed to prefer to look down at us from a long way off, like a llama or a camel.

"Good luck" was what he said to me when they got up to catch the New York train— and Andrea said even less. This time, because we knew each other, she took my hand in five soft fingers, but the touch of the fairy princess seemed to mean much the same to me as the garrison handshake at the faculty-club reception. She's forgotten, I thought, about Knebel. Or maybe she's told Abravanel and figured he'd take care of it, and he's forgotten. Or maybe she's told him and he said, "Forget it." Watching her leave the luncheonette on Abravanel's arm—seeing her hair brush his shoulder as out on the street she rose on her toes to whisper something into his ear—I realized that they'd had other things than my story to think about when they got back to the Windermere the night before.

All of this was why, from Quahsay, I had mailed my four published stories to Lonoff. Felix Abravanel was clearly not in the market for a twenty-three-year-old son.

Just before nine, having checked the time on his watch, Lonoff drank up his last drop of brandy, which had sat thirty minutes at the bottom of the glass. He said that though he must be off, I might stay in the living room and listen to music, or, if I preferred, I could retire to his study, where I would be sleeping. Beneath the corduroy cover I would find that the daybed was already made up with fresh linen. Blankets and an extra pillow were in the closet there, on the bottom shelf, and fresh towels were in the downstairs-bathroom cupboard—please, I mustn't hesitate to use the striped ones, they were the least worn and best for a shower—and also in the cupboard, at the rear of the second shelf, I would find a toothbrush in its original unopened plastic case, and a small new tube of Ipana. Any questions?

"No."

Was there anything else that I would need?

"Thank you, this is all perfect."

He winced when he stood—lumbago, he explained, from turning one too many sentences around that day—and said that he still had his evening's reading. He did not do justice to a writer unless he read him on consecutive days and for no less than three hours at a sitting. Otherwise, despite his notetaking and underlining, he lost touch with a book's inner life and might as well not have begun. Sometimes, when he unavoidably had to miss a day, he would go back and begin all over again, rather than be nagged by his sense that he was wronging a serious author.

He told me all this in the same fastidious way he had described the location of the toothpaste and towels: a blunt, colloquial, pointedly ungrandiloquent Lonoff seemed to take turns with a finicky floorwalker Lonoff as official representative to the unwritten world.

"My wife considers this a grave affliction," he added. "I don't know how to relax. Soon she'll be telling me to go out and have a good time."

"Not that soon," I said.

"It's only as it should be," he said, "for somebody else to think I'm a fool. But I can't afford the luxury myself. How else am I supposed to read a book of real depth? For 'enjoyment'? For the hell of it—to put me to sleep?" Wearily—more ready for bed, I would have thought from the tired, irascible tone, than for one hundred and eighty minutes concentrating on the inner life of a deep book by a serious author—he asked, "How else am I to conduct my life?"

"How else would you like to?"

Well, I had done it, escaped at last from wooden self-consciousness and egregious overearnestness—and sporadic attempts to be witty in the Lonovian mode—and put to him a direct, simple question, the answer to which I wanted very much to hear.

"How else might I like to?"

It thrilled me to see him standing there

taking altogether seriously what I had asked. "Yes. How would you live now, if you had your way?"

Rubbing at the small of his back, he replied, "I would live in a villa outside Florence."

"Yes? With whom?"

"A woman, of course." He answered without hesitation, as though I were another grown man.

So, as though I were one, I went ahead and asked, "How old would she be, this woman?"

He smiled down at me. "We have both had too much to drink."

I showed him that there was brandy enough still to swirl around in my snifter.

"For us," he added, and not bothering this time to catch the trouser crease in his fingers, sat back down somewhat gracelessly in his chair.

"Please," I said, "I don't mean to keep you from reading. I'll be fine alone."

"Sometimes," he said, "I like to imagine I've read my last book. And looked for the last time at my watch. How old would you think she should be?" he asked. "The woman in Florence. As a writer, what would be your guess?"

"I think you'll have to ask me to guess that thirty years from now. I don't know."

"I say thirty-five. How does that strike you?"

"As right, if you say so."

"She would be thirty-five and she would make life beautiful for me. She would make life comfortable and beautiful and new. She would drive me in the afternoon to San Gimignano, to the Uffizi, to Siena. In Siena we would visit the cathedral and drink coffee in the square. At the breakfast table she would wear long feminine nightgowns under her pretty robe. They would be things I had bought for her in a shop by the Ponte Vecchio. I would work in a cool stone room with French windows. There would be flowers in a vase. She would cut them and put them there. And so on, Nathan, in this vein."

Most men want to be children again, or kings, or quarterbacks, or multimillionaires. All Lonoff seemed to want was a thirty-five-year-old woman and a year abroad. I thought of Abravanel, that fruit gatherer, and the Israeli actress—"like lava"—who was Abravanel's third wife. And of that rounded character Andrea Rumbough. In whose sea did Andrea bob now? "If that's all ..." I said.

"Go on. We're having a drunken conversation."

"If that's all, it doesn't sound too hard to arrange," I heard myself telling him.

"Oh, yes? What young woman that you know is out looking for a fifty-six-year-old bald man to accompany to Italy?"

"You're not the stereotypical bald man of fifty-six. Italy with you wouldn't be Italy with anyone."

"What does that mean? I'm supposed to cash in the seven books for a piece of ass?"

The unforeseen plunge into street talk made *me* feel momentarily like the boutonniered floorwalker. "That isn't what I meant. Though of course that happens, such things are done..."

"Yes, in New York you must see a lot of it."

"No one with seven books in New York City settles for one piece of ass. That's what you get for a couplet." I had spoken as though I knew what I was talking about. "All I meant was that you're not exactly asking for a harem."

"Like the fat lady said about the polka-dot dress, 'It's nice, but it's not Lonoff.'"

"Why not?"

"Why not?" he repeated, a little scornfully.

"I meant—why couldn't it be?"

"Why should it be?"

"Because—you want it."

His answer: "Not a good enough reason."

I lacked the courage to ask "Why not?" again. If drunk, still only drunk Jews. So far and no further, I was sure. And I was right.

"No," he said, "you don't chuck a woman out after thirty-five years because you'd prefer to see a new face over your fruit juice."

Thinking of his fiction, I had to wonder if he had ever let her in, or the children either, who, he had told me earlier, had provided him with diversion and brought a certain gaiety into his world for so long as they lived at home. In his seven volumes of stories I could not think of a single hero who was not a bachelor, a widower, an orphan, a foundling, or a reluctant fiancé.

"But there's more to it than that," I said. "More to it than the new face . . . isn't there?"

"What, the bed? I had the bed. I know my singularity," said Lonoff, "and what I owe to it." Here, abruptly, he concluded our drunken conversation. "I've got my reading. Let me show you before I go how to work the phonograph. We have an excellent classical record collection. You know about wiping the records? There is a cloth—"

He came heavily to his feet; slowly and heavily, like an elephant. All the obstinacy seemed to have gone out of him, whether owing to our exchange or to the pain in his back—or exhaustion with his singularity—I didn't know. Maybe every day ended like this.

"Mr. Lonoff—Manny," I said, "may I ask you something before you go, while we're alone—about my stories? I don't know if I entirely understood what you meant by 'turbulence.' At dinner. I don't mean to hang on to one word, but any word from you—well, I'd like to be sure I understand it. That is, I'm thrilled just that you read them, and I'm amazed even to have been invited, and now staying over—all that should be enough. It is enough. And the toast you made"—I felt my emotions getting out of hand, as I had, to my astonishment, while receiving my college diploma with my parents looking on—"I hope I can live up to it. I don't take those words lightly. But about the stories themselves, what I'd like to know is what you think is wrong with them, what you think I might do—to be better?"

How benign was his smile! Even while kneading the lumbago. "Wrong?"

"Yes."

"Look, I told Hope this morning: Zucker-

man has the most compelling voice I've en-
countered in years, certainly for somebody
starting out."

"Do I?"

"I don't mean style"—raising a finger to
make the distinction. "I mean voice: something that begins at around the back of the
knees and reaches well above the head. Don't
worry too much about 'wrong.' Just keep
going. You'll get there."

There. I tried to envision it, but couldn't.
It was more than I could take being *here*.

I told Hope this morning.

Meanwhile, buttoning his jacket and
smoothing down his tie—and checking his
watch with the glance that ruined his wife's
every Sunday—he attended to the last item
of business on the agenda. Working the record player. I had interrupted his train of
thought.

"I want to show you what happens if the
arm doesn't go all the way back at the end
of the record."

"Sure," I said, "absolutely."

"It's been acting up lately and nobody is
able to fix it. Some days it somehow fixes
itself, and then out of the blue it's on the
blink again."

I followed him over to the turntable, thinking less about his classical record collection than about my voice starting back of my knees.

"This is the volume, of course. This is the start button. This is the reject, you push it—"

And this, I realized, is the excruciating scrupulosity, the same maddening, meticulous attention to every last detail that makes you great, that keeps you going and got you through and now is dragging you down. Standing with E. I. Lonoff over the disobedient arm of his record player, I understood the celebrated phenomenon for the first time: a man, his destiny, and his work—all one. What a terrible triumph!

"And," he reminded me, "it would be best for the records, and for your own pleasure, if you remember to wipe them first."

Oh, the fussiness, the fastidiousness! The floorwalker incarnate! To wrestle the blessing of his fiction out of that misfortune— "triumph" didn't begin to describe it.

Suddenly I wanted to kiss him. I know this happens to men more often than is reported, but I was new to manhood (about five minutes into it, actually) and was bewildered by the strength of a feeling that I had rarely had toward my own father once I'd begun to shave. It seemed, at the moment, even stronger than what invariably came over me when I was left alone with those long-necked aerial friends of Betsy's, who walked with their feet turned charmingly outward and looked (just like Betsy!) so appetizingly wan and light and liftable. But in this house of forbearance I was better at suppressing my amorous impulses than I had been lately, unchained in Manhattan.

2

Nathan Dedalus

Who could sleep after that? I didn't even turn the lamp off to try. For the longest time I just stared at E. I. Lonoff's tidy desk: neat piles of typing paper, each stack a different pale color—for different drafts, I assumed. Finally I got up and, sacrilege though it surely was, sat on his typing chair in my undershorts. No wonder his back hurt. It wasn't a chair made for relaxing in, not if you were his size. Lightly I touched my fingers to his portable typewriter keys. Why a portable for a man who went nowhere? Why not a machine on the order of a cannonball, black and big and built to write for all time? Why not a comfortable padded executive's chair to lean back in and think? Why not indeed.

Pinned to the bulletin board beside his desk—the cell's only real embellishments— were a little wall calendar from the local bank and two annotated index cards. One card bore a fragmentary sentence ascribed to "Schumann, on Chopin's Scherzo No. 2 in B flat minor, Op. 31." It read, "... so overflowing with tenderness, boldness, love, and contempt that it may be compared, not inappropriately, to a poem by Byron." I didn't know what to make of it there, or rather, what Lonoff made of it, until I remembered that Amy Bellette could play Chopin with great charm. Maybe it was she who had typed it out for him, scrupulous attribution and all—enclosing it, perhaps, with the gift of a record so that in the late afternoons he could listen to Chopin even when she was no longer around. Perhaps it was this very line she'd been musing upon when I first saw her on the study floor: musing because the description seemed as pertinent to herself as to the music...

If displaced, what had become of her family? Murdered? Did that explain her "contempt"? But for whom the overflowing love, then? Him? If so, the contempt might well be for Hope. If so, if so.

It required no ingenuity to guess the appeal of the quotation typed on the other card. After what Lonoff had been telling me all evening, I could understand why he might want these three sentences hanging over his head while beneath them he sat turning his own sentences around. "We work in the dark—we do what we can—we give what we have. Our doubt is our passion and our passion is our task. The rest is the madness of art." Sentiments ascribed to a story I did not know by Henry James called "The Middle Years." But "the madness of art"? I would have thought the madness of everything but art. The art was what was sane, no? Or was I missing something? Before the night was over I was to read "The Middle Years" twice through, as though preparing to be examined on it in the morning. But that was canon law to me then: ready to write a thousand words on "What does Henry James mean by 'the madness of art'?" if the question should happen to turn up on my paper napkin at breakfast.

Photographs of Lonoff's children were set out on a bookshelf behind the typing chair: one male, two females, not a trace of the paternal genes in any of their bones. One of the girls, a fair, freckled maiden in horn-rimmed glasses, looked, in fact, much as her shy, studious mother probably did back in her art-school days. Beside her photo in the twin frame was a postcard that had been mailed from Scotland to Massachusetts one August day nine years earlier, addressed to the writer alone. This perhaps accounted for its status as a memento to be preserved under glass. Much about his life indicated that communicating with his children had been no easier for him than having enough opinions for Manhattan in the thirties. "Dear Pop, We are now in Banffshire (Highlands) and I am standing amidst the wreck of Balvenie Castle, Dufftown, where Mary Stuart once stayed. Yesterday we biked to Cawdor (Thane of Cawdor, *ca.* 1050, Shakespeare's Macbeth), where Duncan was murdered. See you soon, Love, Becky."

Also directly behind his desk were several shelves of his works in foreign translation. Seating myself on the floor I tried translating from French and German sentences that I had read first in Lonoff's English. With the more exotic tongues the most I could do was try to spot his characters' names in the hundreds of indecipherable pages. Pechter.

Marcus. Littman. Winkler. There they were, surrounded on all sides by Finnish.

And which language was hers? Portuguese? Italian? Hungarian? In which did she overflow like a poem by Byron?

On a large lined pad that I took from my briefcase, a bulging *Bildungsroman* briefcase—ten pounds of books, five obscure magazines, and easily enough paper to write the whole of my first novel if it should happen to come to me while riding back and forth on the bus—I began methodically to list everything on his bookshelves I had not read. There was more German philosophy than I had been expecting, and only halfway down the page I already seemed to have sentenced myself to a lifetime at hard labor. But worthily, I kept going—to the accompaniment of the words with which he had commended me before going up to his reading. That, and the toast, had been echoing in my head for an hour. On a clean sheet of paper I finally wrote down what he'd said so as to see exactly what he'd meant. All he'd meant.

As it turned out, I wanted someone else to see as well, for soon I had forgotten the forthcoming ordeal with Heidegger and Wittgenstein, and was seated with my pad at Lonoff's desk, struggling to explain to my father—the

foot-doctor father, the first of my fathers—
the "voice" that, according to no less a vo-
calist than E. I. Lonoff, started back of my
knees and reached above my head. The letter
was overdue. Three weeks now he had been
waiting for some enlightened sign of contri-
tion for the offenses I had begun to commit
against my greatest supporters. And for three
weeks I had let him stew, if that is how you
describe being yourself unable to think of little else upon awakening from bad dreams at
4 a.m.

Our trouble had begun when I gave my father
the manuscript of a story based on an old
family feud in which he had played peace-
maker for nearly two years before the oppo-
nents ended up shouting in court. The story
was the most ambitious I had written—some
fifteen thousand words—and, as I saw it, my
motives for sending it to him were no less
benign than those I'd had in college, when I
mailed home poems for the family to read
even before they appeared in the student
verse magazine. It wasn't trouble I was looking for but admiration and praise. Out of the
oldest and most ingrained of habits, I wanted
to please them and make them proud.

That wasn't hard either. For years I had

been making him proud just by sending along clippings for his "files," a voluminous accumulation of magazine and newspaper articles—including an unbroken series of transcripts of "America's Town Meeting of the Air"—on what he called "vital issues." Whenever I was home on a visit, my mother, who could repeat herself, would invariably remind me—with her own deeply satisfied look—of the thrill it gave him to say to his patients (after working them around to the vital issue on his mind), "I just got something in the mail this morning on that subject. My son Nathan saw it at college. He's out at the University of Chicago. Straight A's in everything. Went out there when he was sixteen— special program. Well, he saw it in one of the Chicago papers and sent it on for my files."

Oh, what sitting ducks I had for parents! A son of theirs would have had to be a half-wit or a sadist *not* to make them proud. And I was neither; I was dutiful and thoughtful, and too excited with myself in flight to be ungrateful for the boost I'd begun with. Despite the flaming wrangles of my adolescence—weekend night hours, fashions in footwear, the unhygienic high-school hangout, my alleged but ceaselessly disavowed penchant for the last word—we had emerged from our fifty textbook scenes of domestic schism much the same close family bound by the same strong feelings. I'd slammed a lot of doors and declared a few wars, but still I loved them like their child. And whether or not I wholly knew just how extensive the addiction, I was much in need of their love for me, of which I assumed there was an inexhaustible supply. That I couldn't—wouldn't?—assume otherwise goes a long way toward explaining why I was naïve enough to expect nothing more than the usual encouragement for a story that borrowed from our family history instances of what my exemplary father took to be the most shameful and disreputable transgressions of family decency and trust.

The facts I had begun my story with were these:

A great-aunt of mine, Meema Chaya, had left for the education of two fatherless grandsons the pot of money she had diligently hoarded away as a seamstress to Newark's upper crust. When Essie, the widowed mother of the twin boys, attempted to invade the trust to send them from college to medical school, her younger brother, Sidney, who was to inherit the money remaining in Meema Chaya's estate upon conclusion of the boys'

higher education, had sued to stop her. For
four years Sidney had been waiting for Richard and Robert to graduate from Rutgers—
waiting mostly in pool rooms and saloons, to
hear the family tell it—so he could buy a
downtown parking lot with his legacy.
Loudly—his way—Sidney proclaimed that he
was not about to postpone the good life just
so there could be two more fancy doctors driving Caddies around South Orange. Those in
the family who detested Sidney's womanizing
and his shady friends immediately lined up
in support of the boys and their dignified as-
pirations, leaving Sidney with a phalanx con-
sisting of his ill-used, timid wife Jenny, and
his mysterious Polish tootsie Annie, whose
scandalously florid *shmatas* were much discussed, if never once seen, at family wed-
dings, funerals, etc. Also in the phalanx, for
all it was worth to him, was me. My admiration was long-standing, dating back to Sidney's Navy days, when he had won four thousand dollars on the homeward journey of the
battleship *Kansas*, and was said to have
thrown into the South Pacific, for the sharks
to dispose of, a Mississippi sore loser who at
the end of an all-night poker game had referred to the big winner as a dirty Jew. The
lawsuit, whose outcome hinged on how ex-

haustive Meema Chaya had meant to be in her will with the ringing words "higher education," was eventually decided by the judge—a *goy*—in Sidney's favor, though within only a few years the Raymond Boulevard parking lot bought with his inheritance became such a hot piece of real estate that it was nationalized out from under him by the Mob. For his trouble they gave Sidney a tenth of what it was worth, and shortly thereafter his heart broke like a balloon in the bed of yet another overdressed bimbo not of our persuasion. My cousins Richard and Robert were meanwhile being put through medical school by their iron-willed mother. After she lost the lawsuit, Essie quit her job at a downtown department store and for the next ten years went to work on the road selling shingles and siding. So iron-willed was she that by the time she had finally bought carpeting and venetians for the new offices leased for Richard and Robert in suburban North Jersey, there was hardly a working-class neighborhood in the state that she hadn't left encased in asphalt. Out canvassing one hot afternoon during the twins' internship, Essie had decided to spend an hour in an air-cooled Passaic movie theater. In her thousands of days and nights finding leads and closing deals, this was said to be the first time ever that she stopped to do anything other than eat and call the boys. But now residencies in orthopedics and dermatology were only just around the corner, and the thought of their advent, combined with the August heat, made her just a little light-headed. In the dark movie theater, however, Essie hadn't even time to mop her brow before a fellow in the next seat put his hand on her knee. He must have been a very lonely fellow—it was a very stout knee; nonetheless, she broke the hand for him, at the wrist, with the hammer carried in her purse all these years to protect herself and the future of two fatherless sons. My story, entitled "Higher Education," concluded with Essie taking aim.

"Well, you certainly didn't leave anything out, did you?"

Thus began my father's critique on the Sunday I'd come to say goodbye before leaving for the winter at Quahsay. Earlier in the day, along with a favorite aunt and uncle and a childless neighbor couple—also called "Aunt" and "Uncle" by me since the cradle—I had partaken of our family's traditional Sunday brunch. Fifty-two Sundays a year, for most of my lifetime, my father went out to the corner for the smoked fish and the warm rolls, my brother and I set the table and squeezed the juice, and for three hours my mother was unemployed in her own house. "Like a queen" was how she described the predicament. Then, after my parents had read the Newark Sunday papers and listened on the radio to "The Eternal Light"—great moments from Jewish history in weekly half-hour dramatizations—we two boys were rounded up and the four of us set off in the car to visit relatives. My father, long in contention with an opinionated older brother for the vacant position of family patriarch, generally delivered a hortatory sermon somewhere along the way to somebody who seemed to him to need it, and then we drove home. And always at dusk, before we reassembled around the kitchen table to observe the Sunday-evening rites—to partake of the sacred delicatessen supper, washed down with sacramental soda pop; to await together the visitation from heaven of Jack Benny, Rochester, and Phil Harris—the "men," as my mother called us, went off for their brisk walk to the nearby park. "Hi, Doc—how are you?" So the neighbors we passed along the way always greeted my popular and talkative father, and though he seemed never to be bothered by it, for a time his class-conscious little boy used to think that if only there had been no quotas and he'd become a *real* physician, they would have greeted him as "Doctor Zuckerman." "Doc" was what they called the pharmacist who made milk shakes and sold cough drops.

"Well, Nathan," began my father, "you certainly didn't leave anything out, did you?"

I was by then a little weary from doing my duty and anxious to leave for New York to pack for Quahsay. My brunch-time visit had now lasted the entire day and, to my surprise, had been marked by the comings and goings of numerous relatives and old family friends dropping by seemingly just to see me. Kibitzing, reminiscing, swapping dialect jokes, and munching too much fruit, I had hung around until the company began to leave, and then had stayed on, at my father's request, so that he could give me his thoughts on my story. Portentously he said he wanted an hour with me alone.

At four that afternoon, in our coats and scarves, the two of us set out for the park. Every half hour a New York bus stopped just by the park gateway on Elizabeth Avenue, and my plan was to catch one after he'd had his say.

"I left a lot of things out." I pretended to be innocent of what he meant—as innocent as when I'd sent him the story, though the moment he'd spoken in the house of giving me his "thoughts" (rather than his pat on the head), I realized immediately how mindless I had been. Why hadn't I waited to see if I could even get it published, and then shown him the story already in print? Or would that only have made it worse? "Things had to be left out—it's only fifty pages."

"I mean," he said sadly, "you didn't leave anything disgusting out."

"Did I? Didn't I? I wasn't thinking along those lines, exactly."

"You make everybody seem awfully greedy, Nathan."

"But everybody was."

"That's one way of looking at it, of course."

"That's the way you looked at it yourself. That's why you were so upset that they wouldn't compromise."

"The point is, there is far more to our family than this. And you know that. I hope that today reminded you of the kind of people we are. In case in New York you've forgotten."

"Dad, I had a good time seeing everybody. But you didn't have to give me a refresher course in the family's charms."

But on he went. "And people who are crazy about you. Is there anybody who came into the house today whose face didn't light up when they laid eyes on you? And you couldn't have been kinder, you couldn't have been a sweeter boy. I watched you with your family and with all our old dear friends, and I thought to myself, Then what is this story all about? Why is he going on like this about ancient history?"

"It wasn't ancient history when it happened."

"No, then it was nonsense."

"You didn't seem to think so. You were running from Essie to Sidney for over a year."

"The fact remains, son, there is more to the family, much much more, than is in this story. Your great-aunt was as kind and loving and hard-working a woman as you could ever meet in this world. Your grandmother and all her sisters were, every last one of them. They were women who thought only of others."

"But the story is not about them."

"But they are *part* of the story. They are the *whole* story as far as I'm concerned. Without them there would be no story at all! Who the hell was Sidney? Does anybody in his right mind even think about him any longer? To you, as a boy, I suppose he was an amusing character, somebody to get a kick out of, who came and went. I can understand how that would be: a big six-foot ape in bell-bottom trousers, clanking his I.D. bracelet and talking a mile a minute as though he was Admiral Nimitz and not just the nobody who swabbed the deck. Which is all he ever was, of course. I remember how he came to the house and got down on the floor and taught you and your little brother to roll dice. As a joke. I wanted to throw the lummox out on his ear."

"I don't even remember that."

"Well, I do. I remember plenty. I remember it all. To Meema Chaya, Sidney was never anything but heartache. Little children don't realize that underneath the big blowhard who rolls on the floor and makes them laugh there can be somebody who makes other people cry. And he made your great-aunt cry plenty, and from the time he was old enough to go into the street, looking for grief to give her. And still, *still*, that woman left him that chunk of her hard-earned dough, and prayed that somehow it would help. She rose above all the misery and the shame he had caused her—just like the wonderful woman that she was. 'Chaya' means life, and that is what she had in her to give to everybody. But that you leave out."

"I didn't leave it out. I suggest as much about her on the first page. But you're right—I don't go into Meema Chaya's life."

"Well, that would be some story."

"Well, that isn't this story."

"And do you fully understand what a story like this story, when it's published, will mean to people who don't know us?"

We had by now descended the long incline of our street and reached Elizabeth Avenue. No lawn we passed, no driveway, no garage, no lamppost, no little brick stoop was without its power over me. Here I had practiced my sidearm curve, here on my sled I'd broken a tooth, here I had copped my first feel, here for teasing a friend I had been slapped by my mother, here I had learned that my grandfather was dead. There was no end to all I could remember happening to me on this street of one-family brick houses more or less like ours, owned by Jews more or less like us, to whom six rooms with a "finished" basement and a screened-in porch on a street with shade trees was something never to be taken for granted, given the side of the city where they'd started out.

Across the wide thoroughfare was the entrance to the park. There my father used to seat himself—each Sunday the same bench—

to watch my brother and me play tag, yelling our heads off after hours of good behavior with grandparents, great-aunts and great-uncles, ordinary aunts and uncles—sometimes it seemed to me that there were more Zuckermans in Newark than Negroes. I wouldn't see as many of them in a year as I saw cousins on an ordinary Sunday driving around the city with my father. "Oh," he used to say, "how you boys love to shout" and with one hand for each son's head would smooth back our damp hair as we started out of the park and back up the familiar hill where we lived. "Any game with shouting in it," he would tell our mother, "and these two are in seventh heaven." Now my younger brother was knuckling under to the tedium of a pre-dental course, having surrendered (to my father's better judgment) a halfhearted dream of a career as an actor, and I—? I apparently was shouting again.

I said, "I think maybe I'll just get the bus. Maybe we should skip the park. It's been a long day, and I have to go home and get ready to leave for Quahsay tomorrow."

"You haven't answered my question."

"It wouldn't be useful, Dad. The best thing now is to put the story in the mail and send it back to me—and try to forget it."

113

My suggestion triggered a light sardonic laugh from my father.

"All right," I said sharply, "then don't forget it."

"Calm down," he replied. "I'll walk you to the bus. I'll wait with you."

"You really ought to go home. It's getting cold."

"I'm plenty warm," he informed me.

We waited in silence at the bus stop.

"They take their time on Sundays," he finally said. "Maybe you should come home and have dinner. You could catch one first thing in the morning."

"I've got to go to Quahsay first thing in the morning."

"They can't wait?"

"I can't," I said.

I stepped out into the street to watch for the bus.

"You're going to get yourself killed out there."

"Perhaps."

"So," he said, when at last, in my own sweet time, I came back up on the curb, "what do you do with the story now? Send it to a magazine?"

"It's long for a magazine. Probably no magazine will publish it."

"Oh, they'll publish it. The *Saturday Review* has put you on the map. That was a wonderful write-up, a terrific honor to be chosen like that at your age."

"Well, we'll see."

"No, no. You're on your way. The *Saturday Review* never sold so many copies in North Jersey as when your picture was in it. Why do you think everybody came by today, Frieda and Dave, Aunt Tessie, Birdie, Murray, the Edelmans? Because they saw your picture and they're proud."

"They all told me."

"Look, Nathan, let me have my say. Then you can go, and up there at the artists' colony maybe you'll think over in peace and quiet what I'm trying to get you to understand. If you were going to turn out to be nobody, I wouldn't be taking this seriously. But I do take you seriously—and you have to take yourself seriously, and what you are doing. Stop looking for that goddam bus and listen to me, *please*. You can catch the *next* bus! Nathan, you are not in school any more. You are the older brother and you are out in the world and I am treating you accordingly."

"I understand that. But that doesn't mean that we can't disagree. That's what it *does* mean."

"But from a lifetime of experience I happen to know what ordinary people will think when they read something like this story. And you don't. You can't. You have been sheltered from it all your life. You were raised here in this neighborhood where you went to school with Jewish children. When we went to the shore and had the house with the Edelmans, you were always among Jews, even in the summertime. At Chicago your best friends who you brought home were Jewish boys, always. It's not your fault that you don't know what Gentiles think when they read something like this. But I can tell you. They don't think about how it's a great work of art. They don't know about art. Maybe I don't know about art myself. Maybe none of our family does, not the way that you do. But that's my point. People don't read art—they read about *people*. And they judge them as such. And how do you think they will judge the people in your story, what conclusions do you think they will reach? Have you thought about that?"

"Yes."

"And what have you concluded?"

"Oh, I can't put it into one word, not out here in the street. I didn't write fifteen thousand words so as now to put it into one word."

"Well, I can. And the street isn't a bad place for it. Because I know the word. I wonder if you fully understand just how very little love there is in this world for Jewish people. I don't mean in Germany, either, under the Nazis. I mean in run-of-the-mill Americans, Mr. and Mrs. Nice Guy, who otherwise you and I consider perfectly harmless. Nathan, it is there. I guarantee you it is there. I *know* it is there. I have seen it, I have felt it, even when they do not express it in so many words."

"But I'm not *denying* that. Why did Sidney throw that redneck off his ship—?"

"Sidney," he said furiously, "never threw any redneck off any ship! Sidney threw the bull, Nathan! Sidney was a petty hoodlum who cared about nobody and nothing in this world but the good of Sidney!"

"And who actually existed, Dad—and no better than I depict him!"

"Better? He was worse! How rotten he was you don't *begin* to know. I could tell you stories about that bastard that would make your hair stand on end."

"Then where *are* we? If he was *worse*— Oh, look, we're not getting anywhere. Please, it's getting dark, it's going to snow—*go home*. I'll write when I get up there. But there is no more to say on this subject. We just disagree, period."

"All right!" he said crisply, "all right!" But only, I knew, to defuse me for the moment.

"Dad, go home, please."

"It won't hurt if I wait with you. I don't like you waiting out here by yourself."

"I can manage perfectly well out here by myself. I have for years now."

Some five minutes later, blocks away, we saw what looked like the lights of the New York bus.

"Well," I said, "I'll be back down in a few months. I'll keep in touch—I'll phone—"

"Nathan, your story, as far as Gentiles are concerned, is about one thing and one thing only. Listen to me, before you go. It is about kikes. Kikes and their love of money. That is all our good Christian friends will see, I guarantee you. It is not about the scientists and teachers and lawyers they become and the things such people accomplish for others. It is not about the immigrants like Chaya who worked and saved and sacrificed to get a decent footing in America. It is not about the wonderful peaceful days and nights you spent growing up in our house. It is not about the lovely friends you always had. No, it's about Essie and her hammer, and Sidney and

118

his chorus girls, and that shyster of Essie's and his filthy mouth, and, as best I can see, about what a jerk I was begging them to reach a decent compromise before the whole family had to be dragged up in front of a *goyisher* judge."

"I didn't depict you as a jerk. Christ, far from it. I thought," I said angrily, "I was administering a bear hug, to tell you the truth."

"Oh, did you? Well, it didn't come out that way. Look, son, maybe I *was* a jerk, trying to talk sense to such people. I don't mind being made a little fun of—that couldn't bother me less. I've been around in life. But what I can't accept is what you don't see— what you don't *want* to see. This story isn't us, and what is worse, it isn't even *you*. You are a loving boy. I watched you like a hawk all day. I've watched you all your life. You are a good and kind and considerate young man. You are not somebody who writes this kind of story and then pretends it's the truth."

"But I *did* write it." The light changed, the New York bus started toward us across the intersection—and he threw his arms onto my shoulders. Making me all the more belligerent. "I *am* the kind of person who writes this kind of story!"

"You're not," he pleaded, shaking me just a little.

But I hopped up onto the bus, and then behind me the pneumatic door, with its hard rubber edge, swung shut with what I took to be an overly appropriate thump, a symbol of the kind you leave out of fiction. It was a sound that suddenly brought back to me the prize fights at the Laurel Garden, where once a year my brother and I used to wager our pennies with one another, each of us alternately backing the white fighter or the colored fighter, while Doc Zuckerman waved hello to his few acquaintances in the sporting crowd, among them, on one occasion, Meyer Ellenstein, the dentist who became the city's first Jewish mayor. What I heard was the heartrending thud that follows the round-house knockout punch, the sound of the stupefied heavyweight hitting the canvas floor. And what I saw, when I looked out to wave goodbye for the winter, was my small-ish, smartly dressed father—turned out for my visit in a new "fingertip" car coat that matched the coffee-toned slacks and the checkered peaked cap, and wearing, of course, the same silver-rimmed spectacles, the same trim little mustache that I had grabbed at from the crib; what I saw was my bewildered father, alone on the darkening street-corner by the park that used to be our paradise, thinking himself and all of Jewry gratuitously disgraced and jeopardized by my inexplicable betrayal.

Nor was that the end. So troubled was he that several days later, against the counsel of my mother, and after an unpleasant phone conversation with my younger brother, who warned him from Ithaca that I wasn't going to like it when I found out, he decided to seek an audience with Judge Leopold Wapter, after Ellenstein and Rabbi Joachim Prinz perhaps the city's most admired Jew.

Wapter had been born of Galician Jews in the slums adjacent to the city's sweatshops and mills some ten years before our family arrived there from Eastern Europe in 1900. My father still remembered having been rescued by one of the Wapter brothers—it could have been the future jurist himself—when a gang of Irish hooligans were having some fun throwing the seven-year-old mocky up into the air in a game of catch. I had heard this story more than once in my childhood, usually when we drove by the landscaped gardens and turreted stone house on Clinton Avenue where Wapter lived with a spinster daughter—one of the first Jewish students at

Vassar College to earn the esteem of her Christian teachers—and his wife, the department-store heiress, whose philanthropic activities had given her family name the renown among the Jews of Essex County that it was said to have in her native Charleston. Because the Wapters occupied a position of prestige and authority rather like that accorded in our household to President and Mrs. Roosevelt, I used to imagine her, when I was a small boy, going around wearing Mrs. Roosevelt's dowager hats and dresses, and, oddly for a Jewish woman, speaking in the First Lady's awesome Anglified tones. It did not seem to me that, coming from South Carolina, she could really *be* Jewish. Which was exactly what she thought about me, after reading my story.

To approach the judge, my father had first to contact a lofty cousin of ours—an attorney, a suburbanite, and a former Army colonel who had been president for several years of the judge's Newark temple. Cousin Teddy had already helped him to the judge once before, back when my father had gotten it into his head that I should be one of the five youngsters for whom each year Wapter wrote letters of recommendation to college-admissions officers which—it was said—never failed to do the trick. To go up before Judge Wapter I had to wear a blue suit on a bus in broad daylight and then, from where the bus left me off at the Four Corners (our Times Square), to walk all the way up Market Street through throngs of shoppers, whom I imagined dropping in their tracks at the sight of me out in my only dress suit at that hour. I was to be interviewed at the Essex County Courthouse, in his "chambers," a word that had been intoned to relatives on the phone so frequently and with such reverence by my mother during the preceding week that it may well have accounted for the seven visits I made to our bathroom before I could get myself buttoned for good into the blue suit.

Teddy had telephoned the night before to give me some tips on how to conduct myself. This explained the suit and my father's black silk socks, which I was wearing held up with a pair of his garters, and also the initialed briefcase, a grade-school graduation present that I had never removed from the back of my closet. In the gleaming briefcase I carried ten typewritten pages I had written for International Relations the year before on the Balfour Declaration.

As instructed, I "spoke up" right away and offered to show the judge the essay. To my

relief, his chambers had turned out to be one
room, not ten—and a room no more grand
than the principal's office in our high school.
Nor did the tanned, plumpish, cheery judge
have the shock of white hair I had been expecting. And though not as small as my
father, he still was easily a foot shorter than
Abraham Lincoln, whose bronze statue you
pass coming into the courthouse. He actually
looked years younger than my own anxious
father, and not half as serious. Reputedly an
excellent golfer, he was probably either on
his way to or from a game; that's how I later
came to terms with his argyle socks. But
when I first noticed them—as he leaned back
in his leather chair to flip through my essay—I was shocked. It was as though he were
the callow, unworldy applicant, and I, with
my father's garters pulled tight as a tourni-
quet, were the judge. "May I keep this for
now, Nathan?" he asked, turning with a
smile through my pages of *op. cits* and *ibids.*
"I'd like to take it home for my wife to see."
Then began the inquiry. I had prepared myself the night before (at Teddy's suggestion)
by reading through the Constitution of the
United States, the Declaration of Independence, and the editorial page of the Newark
Evening News. The members of Truman's

Cabinet and the majority and minority leaders of both Houses of Congress I of course knew already by heart, though before bed I had gone over them out loud with my mother just to help her relax.

To the judge's questions I gave the following answers:

Journalist. The University of Chicago. Ernie Pyle. One brother, younger. Reading—and sports. The Giants in the National League and the Tigers in the American. Mel Ott and Hank Greenberg. Li'l Abner. Thomas Wolfe. Canada; Washington, D.C.; Rye, New York; New York City itself; Philadelphia; and the Jersey shore. No, sir, never to Florida.

When the judge's secretary made public the names of Newark's five Jewish boys and girls whose college applications Wapter would endorse, mine was one.

I never saw the judge again, though to please my father I had sent my sponsor a letter from the University of Chicago during orientation week of my freshman year, thanking him again for all he had done on my behalf. The letter I received from Wapter some seven years later, during my second week as a guest at Quahsay, was the first I knew of their meeting to talk about "Higher Education."

Philip Roth

Dear Nathan:

My familiarity with your fine family goes back, as you must know, to the turn of the century on Prince Street, where we were all poor people in a new land, struggling for our basic needs, our social and civil rights, and our spiritual dignity. I still remember you as one of the outstanding Jewish graduates of our Newark public-school system. I was most pleased to hear from your father that your college record was at the same high level of achievement that you had maintained throughout your school career here, and that you are already beginning to gain recognition in the field of short-story writing. Since there is nothing a judge likes better than to be right from time to time, I was delighted to know that my confidence in you as a high-school senior has already been substantiated in the larger world. I expect that your family and your community can look forward to great achievements from you in the not too distant future.

Your father, knowing of my interest in the development of our outstanding young people, recently asked if I would take time out from my judicial duties to write you with my candid opinion of one of your short stories. He informed me that you are soon to submit the short story entitled "Higher Education" to a leading national magazine, and he wanted to know whether I thought the story contained material suitable for such a publication.

In our lengthy and interesting conversation here in my chambers, I informed him that classically, down through the ages and in all countries, the artist has always considered himself beyond the mores of the community in which he lived. Great artists, as history reveals, have been harshly persecuted time and again by the frightened and ill-educated, who do not understand that the artist is a special individual with a unique contribution to make to mankind. Socrates was considered an enemy of the people and a corrupter of the young. The Norwegian playwright and Nobel Prize winner, Henrik Ibsen, was forced into exile because his countrymen failed to understand the profound truth of his great dramas. I explained to your father that I for one would never want to be allied with the intolerance shown by the Greeks towards Socrates, or by the Norwegians towards Ibsen. On the other hand, I do believe that, like all men, the artist has a responsibility to his fellow man, to the society in which he lives, and to the cause of truth and justice. With that responsibility and that alone as my criterion, I would attempt to give him an opinion on the suitability for publication in a national magazine of your latest fictional effort.

Attached you will find a questionnaire about

your story, prepared jointly by my wife and myself. Because of Mrs. Wapter's interest in literature and the arts—and because I did not think it fair to rely solely upon my reading—I have taken the liberty of securing her opinion. These are serious and difficult questions to which Mrs. Wapter and I would like you to give just one hour of your time. We don't want you to answer them to our satisfaction—we want you to answer them to your own. You are a young man of great promise and, we all think, of potentially great talent. But with great talent come great responsibilities, and an obligation to those who have stood behind you in the early days so that your talent might come to fruition. I would like to think that if and when the day should dawn that you receive *your* invitation to Stockholm to accept a Nobel Prize, we will have had some small share in awakening your conscience to the responsibilities of your calling.

Sincerely yours,
Leopold Wapter

P.S. If you have not yet seen the Broadway production of *The Diary of Anne Frank*, I strongly advise that you do so. Mrs. Wapter and I were in the audience on opening night; we wish that Nathan Zuckerman could have been with us to benefit from that unforgettable experience.

The sheet of questions prepared for me by the Wapters read as follows:

TEN QUESTIONS FOR NATHAN ZUCKERMAN

1. If you had been living in Nazi Germany in the thirties, would you have written such a story?

2. Do you believe Shakespeare's Shylock and Dickens's Fagin have been of no use to anti-Semites?

3. Do you practice Judaism? If so, how? If not, what credentials qualify you for writing about Jewish life for national magazines?

4. Would you claim that the characters in your story represent a fair sample of the kinds of people that make up a typical contemporary community of Jews?

5. In a story with a Jewish background, what reason is there for a description of physical intimacy between a married Jewish man and an unmarried Christian woman? Why in a story with a Jewish background must there be (a) adultery; (b) incessant fighting within a family over money; (c) warped human behavior in general?

6. What set of aesthetic values makes you think that the cheap is more valid than the noble and the slimy is more truthful than the sublime?

7. What in your character makes you associate so much of life's ugliness with Jewish people?

8. Can you explain why in your story, in which a rabbi appears, there is nowhere the grandeur of oratory with which Stephen S. Wise and Abba Hillel Silver and Zvi Masliansky have stirred and touched their audiences?

9. Aside from the financial gain to yourself, what benefit do you think publishing this story in a national magazine will have for (a) your family; (b) your community; (c) the Jewish religion; (d) the well-being of the Jewish people?

10. Can you honestly say that there is anything in your short story that would not warm the heart of a Julius Streicher or a Joseph Goebbels?

Three weeks after hearing from the judge and Mrs. Wapter, and only days before my visit to Lonoff, I was interrupted around noon by the Colony secretary. She had come out to my cabin in her coat, apologizing for the disturbance, but saying that I had a long-distance phone call that had been described by the other party as an emergency.

When my mother heard my voice she began to cry. "I know it's wrong to bother you," she said, "but I can't take any more. I can't take another night of it. I can't sit through another meal."

"What is it? What's the matter?"

"Nathan, did you or didn't you get a letter from Judge Wapter?"

"Oh, I got it all right."

"But"—she was flabbergasted—"then why didn't you answer it?"

"He should not have gone to Wapter with that story, Mother."

"Oh, darling, maybe he shouldn't. But he did. He did because he knows you respect the judge—"

"I don't even *know* the judge."

"That's not *true*. He did so much for you when you were ready for college. He gave you such a wonderful boost. It turns out that in his files he still had the essay you wrote on the Balfour Declaration in high school. His secretary took out the files and there it was. Daddy saw it, right in his chambers. Why you haven't given him the courtesy of a reply...Daddy is beside himself. He can't believe it."

"He'll have to."

"But all he wanted was for you not to bring yourself harm. You know that."

"I thought it was the harm I was going to do the Jews that you're all worried about."

"Darling, please, for my sake, why won't you answer Judge Wapter? Why won't you give him the hour he asks for? Surely you have an hour where you are to write a letter. Because you cannot, at the age of twenty-three, ignore such a person. You cannot make enemies at twenty-three of people who are so admired and loved, and by Gentiles, too."

"Is that what my father says?"

"He says so much, Nathan. It's been three *weeks* now."

"And how does he even know I haven't answered?"

"From Teddy. He didn't hear from you, so finally he called him. You can well imagine. Teddy is a little fit to be tied. He's not used to this treatment, either. After all, he also extended himself on our behalf when you wanted to go to Chicago."

"Ma, I hate to suggest this, but it could be that the judge's famous letter, procured after great ass-kissing all around, had about as much effect on the University of Chicago as a letter about my qualifications from Rocky Graziano."

"Oh, Nathan, where's your humility,

where's your modesty—where's the courtesy you have always had?"

"Where are my father's *brains!*"

"He only wants to *save* you."

"From what?"

"Mistakes."

"Too late, Mother. Didn't you read the Ten Questions for Nathan Zuckerman?"

"Dear, I did. He sent us a copy—and the letter, too."

"The Big Three, Mama! Streicher, Goebbels, and your son! What about the *judge's* humility? Where's *his* modesty?"

"He only meant that what happened to the Jews—"

"In Europe—not in Newark! We are not the wretched of Belsen! We were not the victims of that crime!"

"But we *could* be—in their place we *would* be. Nathan, violence is nothing new to Jews, you *know* that!"

"Ma, you want to see physical violence done to the Jews of Newark, go to the office of the plastic surgeon where the girls get their noses fixed. That's where the Jewish blood flows in Essex County, that's where the blow is delivered—with a mallet! To their bones—and to their pride!"

"Please don't shout at me. I'm not up to all of this, please—that's why I'm calling. Judge Wapter did not mean *you* were Goebbels. God forbid. He was only a little shocked still from reading your story. We all were, you can understand that."

"Oh, maybe then you all shock a little too easily. Jews are heirs to greater shocks than I can possibly deliver with a story that has a sharpie in it like Sidney. Or Essie's hammer. Or Essie's lawyer. You know as much yourself. You just *said* as much."

"Oh, darling, then tell the judge that. Just tell him that, the way you told it to me, and that'll do it. Your father will be happy. Write him *something*. You can write such wonderful and beautiful letters. When Grandma was dying, you wrote her a letter that was like a poem. It was like—like listening to French, it was so beautiful. What you wrote about the Balfour Declaration was so beautiful when you were only fifteen years old. The judge gave it back to Daddy and said he still remembered how much it had impressed him. He's not against you, Nathan. But if you get your back up and show disrespect, then he will be. And Teddy too, who could be such a help."

"Nothing I could write Wapter would convince him of anything. Or his wife."

"You could tell him you went to see *The Diary of Anne Frank*. You could at least do that."

"I didn't see it. I read the book. *Everybody* read the book."

"But you liked it, didn't you?"

"That's not the issue. How can you *dis*like it? Mother, I will not prate in platitudes to please the adults!"

"But if you just said that, about reading the book, and liking it . . . Because Teddy told Daddy—well, Nathan, is this true?—that to him it looks like you don't really like Jews very much."

"No, Teddy's got it confused. It's him I don't like very much."

"Oh, darling, don't be clever. Don't start that last word business, please. Just answer me, I'm so confused in the middle of all this. Nathan, tell me something."

"What?"

"I'm only quoting Teddy. Darling . . ."

"What is it, Ma?"

"Are you really anti-Semitic?"

"I'll leave it to you. What do you think?"

"Me? I never heard of such a thing. But Teddy..."

"I know, he's a college graduate and lives with wall-to-wall carpeting in Millburn. But they come pretty stupid too."

"Nathan!"

"Sorry, but that's my opinion."

"Oh, I don't know anything any more—all this from that story! Please, if you will not do anything else I ask, at least phone your father. He's been waiting for something for three whole weeks now. And he's a doer, your father, he's not a man who knows how to wait. Darling, phone him at his office. Phone him now. For me."

"No."

"I beg of you."

"No."

"Oh, I can't believe this is you."

"It *is* me!"

"But—what about your father's love?"

"I am on my own!"

In Lonoff's study that night I began letter after letter explaining myself to my father, but each time I got to the point of repeating E. I. Lonoff's praise for my work, I tore the thing up in a rage. I owed no explanations, and he wouldn't buy those I offered anyway, if he even understood them. Because my voice started back of my knees and reached above my head wasn't going to make him any happier about my informing on those unsavory family miscreants who were nobody's business but our own. Nor would it help to argue that Essie wielding her hammer came off in my story as something more impressive than an embarrassment; that wasn't what other people were going to say about a woman who behaved like that, and then expressed herself in a court of law like a man in a barroom brawl. Nor would a spin through the waxworks of my literary museum—from Babel's Odessa gangsters to Abravanel's Los Angeles worldlings—convince him that I was upholding the responsibilities placed on me by his hero, the judge. Odessa? Why not Mars? He was talking about what people would say when they read that story in North Jersey, where we happened to come from. He was talking about the *goyim*, who looked down on us with enough unearned contempt already, and who would be only too pleased to call us all kikes because of what I had written for the whole world to read about Jews fighting over money. It was not for me to leak the news that such a thing could possibly happen.

That was worse than informing—that was collaborating.

Oh, this is useless, I thought, this is idiotic—and tore up yet another half-finished letter in my defense. That the situation between us had deteriorated so rapidly—by his going to Wapter with my story, and by my refusal to justify myself to my elders—was as it had to be, sooner or later. Hadn't Joyce, hadn't Flaubert, hadn't Thomas Wolfe, the romantic genius of my high-school reading list, all been condemned for disloyalty or treachery or immorality by those who saw themselves as slandered in their works? As even the judge knew, literary history was in part the history of novelists infuriating fellow countrymen, family, and friends. To be sure, our dispute hadn't achieved the luster of literary history quite yet, but still, writers weren't writers, I told myself, if they didn't have the strength to face the insolubility of that conflict and go on.

But what about sons? It wasn't Flaubert's father or Joyce's father who had impugned me for my recklessness—it was my own. Nor was it the Irish he claimed I had maligned and misrepresented, but the Jews. Of which I was one. Of which, only some five thousand days past, there had been millions more.

Yet each time I tried again to explain my motives, the angrier with him I became. It's you who humiliated yourself—now live with it, you moralizing ass! Wapter, that know-nothing windbag! That dopey pillar! And the pious belle with her love for the arts! Worth ten million and she chides *me* about "financial gain"! And Abba Hillel Silver on top of that! Oh, don't waste time on prodigal me about Rabbi Silver's grandeur, lady, tell my late cousin Sidney and his friends in the Mob—quote Zvi Masliansky to them, like you do at the country club on the eighteenth hole!

At around eleven I heard the town snowplow clearing the unpaved road beyond the apple orchard. Later a pickup truck with a snowblade clamped to the front end charged into the driveway and shoved the evening's snowfall into the orchard atop the snowfall of the previous thirty nights. The little Renault arrived last, swerving slowly into the driveway about half an hour later, one beam on high, the other dim, and with half-dead windshield wipers.

At the first sound of her car returning, I had flipped off all my lights and crawled to the study window on my knees so as to watch her make her way toward the house. For I had not stayed awake simply because I

139

couldn't forget my father's disapproval or E. I. Lonoff's toast—I also had no intention of being unconscious when the enchanting and mysterious houseguest (all the more alluring, of course, as Hope's imagined erotic rival) got back to change into her nightdress on the floor above me. What I would be able to do about this, I had no idea. However, just to be awake and unclothed in one bed while she was awake and nearly unclothed in another was better than nothing. It was a start.

But predictably, it was worse than nothing and the start of little that was new. The lantern on the half-buried lamppost between the house and the car shed went dark, and then, from where I was kneeling beside the study door, I heard her enter the house. She moved through the hallway and up the carpeted stairs—and that was the last of her that I saw or heard until about an hour later, when I was privileged to audit another astounding course, this one in the adult evening division of the Lonoff School of the Arts. The rest of what I'd been waiting up for I had, of course, to imagine. But that is easier work by far than making things up at the typewriter. For that kind of imagining you don't have to have your picture in the *Saturday Review*. You don't even have to know the alphabet. Being young will usually get a fellow through with flying colors. You don't even have to be young. You don't have to be anything.

Virtuous reader, if you think that after intercourse all animals are sad, try masturbating on the daybed in E. I. Lonoff's study and see how you feel when it's over. To expiate my sense of utter shabbiness, I immediately took to the high road and drew from Lonoff's bookshelves the volume of Henry James stories containing "The Middle Years," the source of one of the two quotations pinned to the bulletin board. And there where I had indulged myself in this most un-Jamesian lapse from the amenities, I read the story two times through, looking to discover what I could about the doubt that's the writer's passion, the passion that's his task, and the madness of—of all things—art.

Dencombe, a novelist "who had a reputation," is convalescing from a debilitating ailment at an English health resort when a copy of his latest book, *The Middle Years*, arrives from his publisher. Seated alone on a bench looking out to sea, Dencombe reluctantly opens the book—to discover what he believes is the artistic distinction that had always evaded him. His genius has flowered, however, just when he no longer has the strength to develop a "'last manner'... to which his real treasure would be gathered." That would require a second existence, and everything tells him that the first one is nearly over.

While fearfully contemplating the end of his life, Dencombe is joined on the bench by a garrulous young stranger carrying his own copy of *The Middle Years*. He begins to speak ardently of Dencombe's achievement to the mild gentleman who he finds has also been reading the new novel. The admirer—"the greatest admirer... whom it was supposable he might boast"—is Dr. Hugh, physician to a rich, eccentric English countess who is at the hotel, like Dencombe, to recover from some grave illness. Inflamed with passion for *The Middle Years,* Dr. Hugh opens the book to read aloud a particularly beautiful passage; but, having mistakenly seized Dencombe's copy rather than his own, he discovers that the printed text has been altered in a dozen places by a pencil. With this, the anonymous and ailing author on the brink of being discovered—"a passionate corrector" never able to arrive at a final form—feels his sickness sweeping over him and loses consciousness.

In the days that follow, Dencombe, bedridden, hopes that some remedy miraculously

concocted by the attentive young physician
will restore his strength. However, when he
learns that the countess plans to disinherit
Dr. Hugh of a magnificent fortune if he con-
tinues to neglect her for the novelist, Dencombe encourages Dr. Hugh to follow her to
London. But Dr. Hugh cannot overcome his
passionate idolatry, and by the time he acts
on Dencombe's advice to hurry to his em-
ployer, he has already suffered "a terrible in-
jury" for which Dencombe almost believes
himself to be responsible: the countess has
died, in a relapse brought on by her jealousy,
bequeathing to the young physician not a
penny. Says Dr. Hugh, returning from her
grave to the dying soul whom he adores, "I
had to choose."

"You chose to let a fortune go?"

"I chose to accept, whatever they might be, the
consequences of my infatuation," smiled Doctor
Hugh. Then, as a larger pleasantry: "The fortune
be hanged! It's your own fault if I can't get your
things out of my head."

A thin black line had been drawn beneath
the "pleasantry" in Lonoff's book. In script
so tiny it was almost unreadable, the writer

had noted beside it a droll pleasantry of his own: "And also your fault if I can."

From there on, down both margins of the final page describing Dencombe's death, Lonoff had penned three vertical lines. Nothing resembling drollery here. Rather, the six surgically precise black lines seemed to simulate the succession of fine impressions that James's insidious narrative about the novelist's dubious wizardry had scored upon Lonoff's undeluded brain.

After Dencombe has learned the consequences of the young man's infatuation—consequences so utterly irreconcilable with his own honorable convictions that, upon hearing of his place in it all, Dencombe utters "a long bewildered moan"—he lies "for many hours, many days . . . motionless and absent."

At the last he signed to Doctor Hugh to listen and, when he was down on his knees by the pillow, brought him very near. "You've made me think it all a delusion."

"Not your glory, my dear friend," stammered the young man.

"Not my glory—what there is of it! It *is* glory—to have been tested, to have had our little quality and cast our little spell. The thing is to have made somebody care. You happen to be crazy of course, but that doesn't affect the law."

"You're a great success!" said Doctor Hugh, putting into his young voice the ring of a marriage-bell.

Dencombe lay taking this in; then he gathered strength to speak once more. "A second chance—*that's* the delusion. There never was to be but one. We work in the dark—we do what we can—we give what we have. Our doubt is our passion and our passion is our task. The rest is the madness of art."

"If you've doubted, if you've despaired, you've always 'done' it," his visitor subtly argued.

"We've done something or other," Dencombe conceded.

"Something or other is everything. It's the feasible. It's *you*!"

"Comforter!" poor Dencombe ironically sighed.

"But it's true," insisted his friend.

"It's true. It's frustration that doesn't count."

"Frustration's only life," said Doctor Hugh.

"Yes, it's what passes." Poor Dencombe was barely audible, but he had marked with the words the virtual end of his first and only chance.

Within moments of hearing muffled voices coming from above my head, I stood up on

the daybed—my finger still holding my place
in the book—and, stretching to my full height,
tried to make out what was being said up
there and by whom. When that didn't help,
I thought of climbing onto Lonoff's desk; it
was easily a foot or so higher than the daybed
and would put my ear only inches from the
room's low ceiling. But if I should fall, if I
should alter by a millimeter the placement
of his typing paper, if somehow I should leave
footprints—no, I couldn't risk it and shouldn't
even have been thinking of it. I had gone far
enough already by expropriating the corner
of the desk to compose my half dozen unfin-
ished letters home. My sense of propriety, not
to mention the author's gracious hospitality,
required me to restrain myself from commit-
ting such a sordid, callow little indecency.

But in the meantime I had done it.

A woman was crying. Which one, over
what, who was there comforting her—or
causing the tears? Just a little higher and
maybe I could find out. A thick dictionary
would have been perfect, but Lonoff's Web-
ster's was down on a shelf of fat reference
books level with the typing chair, and the
best I could manage under pressure was to
gain another couple of inches by kneeling to

insert between the desk and my feet the volume of stories by Henry James.

Ah, the unreckoned consequences, the unaccountable uses of art! Dencombe would understand. James would understand. But would Lonoff? *Don't fall.*

"Now you're being sensible." Lonoff was the speaker. "You had to see for yourself, and so you saw."

A light thud directly overhead. Someone had dropped into a chair. The weary writer? In his bathrobe now, or still in suit and tie and polished shoes?

Then I heard Amy Bellette. And what was *she* wearing at this hour? "I saw nothing—only more misery either way. Of course I can't live here—but I can't keep living there, either. I can't live anywhere. I can't *live.*"

"Quiet down. She's had it for today. Let her rest, now that she's asleep."

"She's ruining everyone's life."

"Don't blame her for what you hold against me. I'm the one who says no around here. Now *you* go to sleep."

"I can't. I don't want to. We can talk."

"We've talked."

Silence. Were they down on their knees listening through the old floorboards for *me?*

Then they had long since heard my drumming heart.

Bedsprings! Lonoff climbing in beside her!

But it was Amy getting out of bed I heard, not Lonoff climbing in. Her feet lightly crossed the floor only inches above my lips.

"I love you. I love you so, Dad-da. There's no one else like you. They're all such dopes."

"You're a good girl."

"Let me sit on your lap. Just hold me a little and I'll be fine."

"You're fine now. You're always fine in the end. You're the great survivor."

"No, just the world's strongest weakling. Oh, tell me a story. Sing me a song. Oh, imitate the great Durante, I really need it tonight."

At first it sounded like somebody coughing. But then I could hear that, yes, he was singing to her, very quietly, in the manner of Jimmy Durante—"So I ups to him, and he ups to me"—I could catch just the one line, but that was enough for me to recall the song itself being sung by Durante on his radio show, in the celebrated raffish voice, and with the hoarse, endearing simplehearted delivery that the famous author was now impersonating overhead.

"More," said Amy.

Was she now on his lap? Amy in her nightie and Lonoff in his suit?

"You go to sleep," he told her.

"More. Sing 'I Can Do Without Broadway.'"

"'Oh, I know don well I can do widout Broadway—*but* . . . can Broadway do widout meeeee? . . .'"

"Oh, Manny, we could be so happy—in Florence, my sweetest, we could come out of hiding."

"We're not in hiding. We never have been."

"No, not when it's like this. But otherwise it's all so false and wrong and lonely. We could make each other so happy. I wouldn't be your little girl over there. I would when we played, but otherwise I'd be your wife."

"We'd be what we've always been. Stop dreaming."

"No, not so. Without her—"

"You want a corpse on your conscience? She would be dead in a year."

"But I have a corpse on my conscience." The floor creaked where her two feet had suddenly landed. So she *had* been on his lap! "Look!"

"Cover yourself."

"My corpse."

Scuffling on the floorboards. The heavy tread of Lonoff on the move.

"Good night."

"Look at it."

"Melodrama, Amy. Cover up."

"You prefer tragedy?"

"Don't wallow. You're not convincing. Decide not to lose hold—and then don't."

"But I'm going crazy! I cannot live apart from you! I don't know how. Oh, why didn't I take that job—and move back! And the hell with her!"

"You did the right thing. You know just what to do."

"Yes, give things up!"

"Dreamy things, correct."

"Oh, Manny, would it kill you just to kiss my breasts? Is that dreamy, too? Would it cause the death of anyone if you just did that?"

"You cover yourself now."

"Dad-da, *please.*"

But next I heard Lonoff's carpet slippers— yes, he was out of his suit, dressed for bed— padding through the upstairs corridor. Soundlessly as I could, I slipped down from the desk and made my way on my toes to the daybed, where, from the sheer physical effort that had gone into my acrobatic eavesdropping, I collapsed. My astonishment at what I'd overheard, my shame at the unpardonable breach of his trust, my relief at having escaped undiscovered—all that turned out to be nothing, really, beside the frustration I soon began to feel over the thinness of my imagination and what that promised for the future. Dad-da, Florence, the great Durante; her babyishness and desire, his mad, heroic restraint— Oh, if only I could have imagined the scene I'd overheard! If only I could invent as presumptuously as real life! If one day I could just *approach* the originality and excitement of what actually goes on! But if I ever did, what then would they think of me, my father and his judge? How would my elders hold up against that? And if they couldn't, if the blow to their sentiments was finally too wounding, just how well would I hold up against being hated and reviled and disowned?

3

Femme Fatale

It was only a year earlier that Amy had told Lonoff her whole story. Weeping hysterically, she had phoned him one night from the Biltmore Hotel in New York; as best he could understand, that morning she had come down alone on a train from Boston to see the matinee performance of a play, intending to return home again by train in the evening. Instead, after coming out of the theater she had taken a hotel room, where ever since she had been "in hiding."

At midnight, having only just finished his

evening's reading and gone up to bed, Lonoff got into his car and drove south. By four he had reached the city, by six she had told him that it was the dramatization of Anne Frank's diary she had come to New York to see, but it was midmorning before she could explain even somewhat coherently her connection with this new Broadway play.

"It wasn't the play—I could have watched that easily enough if I had been alone. It was the people watching with me. Carloads of women kept pulling up to the theater, women wearing fur coats, with expensive shoes and handbags. I thought, This isn't for me. The billboards, the photographs, the marquee, I could take all that. But it was the women who frightened me—and their families and their children and their homes. Go to a movie, I told myself, go instead to a museum. But I showed my ticket, I went in with them, and of course it happened. It had to happen. It's what happens there. The women cried. Everyone around me was in tears. Then at the end, in the row behind me, a woman screamed, 'Oh, no.' That's why I came running here. I wanted a room with a telephone in it where I could stay until I'd found my father. But all I did once I was here was sit in the bathroom thinking that if he knew, if I told him, then they would have to come out on the stage after each performance and announce, 'But she is really alive. You needn't worry, she survived, she is twenty-six now, and doing very well.' I would say to him, 'You must keep this our secret—no one but you must ever know.' But suppose he was found out? What if we both were? Manny, I couldn't call him. And I knew I couldn't when I heard that woman scream 'Oh, no.' I knew then what's been true all along: I'll never see him again. I have to be dead to everyone."

Amy lay on the rumpled bed, wrapped tightly in a blanket, while Lonoff listened in silence from a chair by the window. Upon entering the unlocked room, he had found her sitting in the empty bathtub, still wearing her best dress and her best coat: the coat because she could not stop trembling, in the tub because it was the farthest she could get from the window, which was twenty floors above the street.

"How pathetic, you must think. What a joke," she said.

"A joke? On whom? I don't see the joke."

"My telling this to you."

"I still don't get it."

"Because it's like one of your stories. An

E. I. Lonoff story . . . called . . . oh, you'd know what to call it. You'd know how to tell it in three pages. A homeless girl comes from Europe, sits in the professor's class being clever, listens to his records, plays his daughter's piano, virtually grows up in his house, and then one day, when the waif is a woman and out on her own, one fine day in the Biltmore Hotel, she casually announces..."

He left his chair and came to sit beside her on the bed while she went to pieces again. "Yes," he said, "quite casually."

"Manny, I'm not a lunatic, I'm not a crackpot, I'm not some girl—you must believe me—trying to be interesting and imitate your art!"

"My dear friend," he replied, his arms around her now and rocking her like a child, "if this is all so—"

"Oh, Dad-da, I'm afraid it really is."

"Well, then, you have left my poor art far behind."

This is the tale that Amy told the morning after she had gone alone to the Cort Theatre to sit amid the weeping and inconsolable audience at the famous New York production of *The Diary of Anne Frank*. This is the story that the twenty-six-year-old young woman with the striking face and the fetching accent and the felicitous prose style and the patience, according to Lonoff, of a Lonoff, expected him to believe was true.

After the war she had become Amy Bellette. She had not taken the new name to disguise her identity—as yet there was no need—but, as she imagined at the time, to forget her life. She had been in a coma for weeks, first in the filthy barracks with the other ailing and starving inmates, and then in the squalid makeshift "infirmary." A dozen dying children had been rounded up by the SS and placed beneath blankets in a room with twelve beds in order to impress the Allied armies advancing upon Belsen with the amenities of concentration-camp living. Those of the twelve still alive when the British got there had been moved to an army field hospital. It was here that she finally came around. She understood sometimes less and sometimes more than the nurses explained to her, but she would not speak. Instead, without howling or hallucinating, she tried to find a way to believe that she was somewhere in Germany, that she was not yet sixteen, and that her family was dead. Those were the facts; now to grasp them.

"Little Beauty" the nurses called her—a silent, dark, emaciated girl—and so, one morning, ready to talk, she told them that the surname was Bellette. Amy she got from an American book she had sobbed over as a child, *Little Women*. She had decided, during her long silence, to finish growing up in America now that there was nobody left to live with in Amsterdam. After Belsen she figured it might be best to put an ocean the size of the Atlantic between herself and what she needed to forget.

She learned of her father's survival while waiting to get her teeth examined by the Lonoff's family dentist in Stockbridge. She had been three years with foster families in England, and almost a year as a freshman at Athene College, when she picked an old copy of *Time* out of the pile in the waiting room and, just turning pages, saw a photograph of a Jewish businessman named Otto Frank. In July of 1942, some two years after the beginning of the Nazi occupation, he had taken his wife and his two young daughters into hiding. Along with another Jewish family, the Franks lived safely for twenty-five months in a rear upper story of the Amsterdam building where he used to have his business offices. Then, in August 1944, their whereabouts were apparently betrayed by one of the workers in the warehouse below, and the hideout was uncovered by the police. Of the eight who'd been together in the sealed-off attic rooms, only Otto Frank survived the concentration camps. When he came back to Amsterdam after the war, the Dutch family who had been their protectors gave him the notebooks that had been kept in hiding by his younger daughter, a girl of fifteen when she died in Belsen: a diary, some ledgers she wrote in, and a sheaf of papers emptied out of her briefcase when the Nazis were ransacking the place for valuables. Frank printed and circulated the diary only privately at first, as a memorial to his family, but in 1947 it was published in a regular edition under the title *Het Achterhuis*—"The House Behind." Dutch readers, *Time* said, were greatly affected by the young teenager's record of how the hunted Jews tried to carry on a civilized life despite their deprivations and the terror of discovery.

Alongside the article—"A Survivor's Sorrows"—was the photograph of the diarist's father, "now sixty." He stood alone in his coat and hat in front of the building on the Prinsengracht Canal where his late family had improvised a last home.

Next came the part of her story that Lonoff

was bound to think improbable. She herself, however, could not consider it all that strange that she should be thought dead when in fact she was alive; nobody who knew the chaos of those final months—the Allies bombing everywhere, the SS in flight—would call that improbable. Whoever claimed to have seen her dead of typhus in Belsen had either confused her with her older sister, Margot, or had figured that she was dead after seeing her so long in a coma, or had watched her being carted away, as good as dead, by the Kapos.

"Belsen was the third camp," Amy told him. "We were sent first to Westerbork, north of Amsterdam. There were other children around to talk to, we were back in the open air—aside from being frightened it really wasn't that awful. Daddy lived in the men's barracks, but when I got sick he managed somehow to get into the women's camp at night and to come to my bed and hold my hand. We were there a month, then we were shipped to Auschwitz. Three days and three nights in the freight cars. Then they opened the doors and that was the last I saw of him. The men were pushed in one direction, we were pushed in the other. That was early September. I saw my mother last at the end of October. She could hardly speak by then. When Margot and I were shipped from Auschwitz, I don't even know if she understood."

She told him about Belsen. Those who had survived the cattle cars lived at first in tents on the heath. They slept on the bare ground in rags. Days went by without food or fresh water, and after the autumn storms tore the tents from their moorings, they slept exposed to the wind and rain. When at last they were being moved into barracks, they saw ditches beyond the camp enclosure piled high with bodies—the people who had died on the heath from typhus and starvation. By the time winter came, it seemed as if everyone still alive was either sick or half mad. And then, while watching her sister slowly dying, she grew sick herself. After Margot's death, she could hardly remember the women in the barracks who had helped her, and knew nothing of what happened to them.

It was not so improbable either that after her long hospital convalescence she had not made her way to the address in Switzerland where the family had agreed to meet if they should ever lose touch with one another. Would a weak sixteen-year-old girl undertake a journey requiring money, visas—re-

quiring hope—only to learn at the other end
that she was as lost and alone as she feared?

No, no, the improbable part was this: that
instead of telephoning *Time* and saying, "I'm
the one who wrote the diary—find Otto
Frank!" she jotted down in her notebook the
date on the magazine's cover and, after a
tooth had been filled, went off with her school
books to the library. What was improbable—
inexplicable, indefensible, a torment still to
her conscience—was that, calm and studious
as ever, she checked *The New York Times
Index* and *Readers' Guide to Periodical Literature* for "Frank, Anne" and "Frank, Otto"
and *"Het Achterhuis,"* and, when she found
nothing, went down to the library's lowest
stacks, where the periodicals were shelved.
There she spent the remaining hour before
dinner rereading the article in *Time*. She
read it until she knew it by heart. She studied
her father's photograph. Now sixty And
those were the words that did it—made of her
once again the daughter who cut his hair for
him in the attic, the daughter who did her
lessons there with him as her tutor, the
daughter who would run to his bed and cling
to him under the covers when she heard the
Allied bombers flying over Amsterdam: suddenly she was the daughter for whom he had

taken the place of everything she could no longer have. She cried for a very long time. But when she went to dinner in the dormitory, she pretended that nothing catastrophic had once again happened to Otto Frank's Anne.

But then right from the beginning she had resolved not to speak about what she had been through. Resolutions were her strong point as a young girl on her own. How else could she have lasted on her own? One of the thousand reasons she could not bear Uncle Daniel, the first of her foster fathers in England, was that sooner or later he wound up telling whoever walked into the house about all that had happened to Amy during the war. And then there was Miss Giddings, the young teacher in the school north of London who was always giving the orphaned little Jewess tender glances during history class. One day after school Miss Giddings took her for a lemon-curd tart at the local tearoom and asked her questions about the concentration camps. Her eyes filled with tears as Amy, who felt obliged to answer, confirmed the stories she had heard but could never quite believe. "Terrible," Miss Giddings said, "so terrible." Amy silently drank her tea and ate her lovely tart, while Miss Giddings, like one of her own history students, tried in vain to understand the past. "Why is it," the unhappy teacher finally asked, "that for centuries people have hated you Jews?" Amy rose to her feet. She was stunned. "Don't ask me that!" the girl said—"ask the madmen who hate us!" And she had nothing further to do with Miss Giddings as a friend—or with anyone else who asked her anything about what they couldn't possibly understand.

One Saturday only a few months after her arrival in England, vowing that if she heard another plaintive "Belsen" out of Uncle Daniel's mouth she would run off to Southampton and stow away on an American ship—and having had about enough of the snooty brand of sympathy the pure-bred English teachers offered at school—she burned her arm while ironing a blouse. The neighbors came running at the sound of her screams and rushed her to the hospital emergency room. When the bandage was removed, there was a patch of purple scar tissue about half the size of an egg instead of her camp number.

After the accident, as her foster parents called it, Uncle Daniel informed the Jewish Welfare Board that his wife's ill health made it impossible for them to continue to have Amy in their home. The foster child moved on to another family—and then another. She told whoever asked that she had been evacuated from Holland with a group of Jewish schoolchildren the week before the Nazis invaded. Sometimes she did not even say that the schoolchildren were Jewish, an omission for which she was mildly rebuked by the Jewish families who had accepted responsibility for her and were troubled by her lying. But she could not bear them all laying their helpful hands upon her shoulders because of Auschwitz and Belsen. If she was going to be thought exceptional, it would not be because of Auschwitz and Belsen but because of what she had made of herself since.

They were kind and thoughtful people, and they tried to get her to understand that she was not in danger in England. "You needn't feel frightened or threatened in any way," they assured her. "Or ashamed of anything." "I'm not ashamed. That's the point." "Well, that isn't always the point when young people try to hide their Jewish origins." "Maybe it isn't with others," she told them, "but it is with me."

On the Saturday after discovering her father's photograph in *Time*, she took the morning bus to Boston, and in every foreign bookstore looked in vain for a copy of *Het*

Achterhuis. Two weeks later she traveled the three hours to Boston again, this time to the main post office to rent a box. She paid for it in cash, then mailed the letter she was carrying in her handbag, along with a money order for fifteen dollars, to Contact Publishers in Amsterdam, requesting them to send, postage paid, to Pilgrim International Bookshop, P.O. Box 152, Boston, Mass., U.S.A., as many copies as fifteen dollars would buy of *Het Achterhuis* by Anne Frank.

She had been dead for him some four years; believing her dead for another month or two would not really hurt much more. Curiously she did not hurt more either, except in bed at night when she cried and begged forgiveness for the cruelty she was practicing on her perfect father, now sixty.

Nearly three months after she had sent the order off to her Amsterdam publisher, on a warm, sunny day at the beginning of August, there was a package too large for the Pilgrim Bookshop post-office box waiting to be picked up in Boston. She was wearing a beige linen skirt and a fresh white cotton blouse, both ironed the night before. Her hair, cut in pageboy style that spring, had been washed and set the previous night, and her skin was evenly tanned. She was swimming a mile

165

every morning and playing tennis every afternoon and, all in all, was as fit and energetic as a twenty-year-old could be. Maybe that was why, when the postal clerk handed her the parcel, she did not tear at the string with her teeth or faint straightaway onto the marble floor. Instead, she walked over to the Common—the package mailed from Holland swinging idly from one hand—and wandered along until she found an unoccupied bench. She sat first on a bench in the shade, but then got up and walked on until she found a perfect spot in the sunshine.

After thoroughly studying the Dutch stamps—postwar issues new to her—and contemplating the postmark, she set about to see how carefully she could undo the package. It was a preposterous display of unruffled patience and she meant it to be. She was feeling at once triumphant and giddy. Forbearance, she thought. Patience. Without patience there is no life. When she had finally untied the string and unfolded, without tearing, the layers of thick brown paper, it seemed to her that what she had so meticulously removed from the wrappings and placed onto the lap of her clean and pretty American girl's beige linen skirt was her survival itself.

Van Anne Frank. Her book. Hers.

She had begun keeping a diary less than three weeks before Pim told her that they were going into hiding. Until she ran out of pages and had to carry over onto office ledgers, she made the entries in a cardboard-covered notebook that he'd given her for her thirteenth birthday. She still remembered most of what happened to her in the achterhuis, some of it down to the most minute detail, but of the fifty thousand words recording it all, she couldn't remember writing one. Nor could she remember anything much of what she'd confided there about her personal problems to the phantom confidante she'd named Kitty—whole pages of her tribulations as new and strange to her as her native tongue.

Perhaps because *Het Achterhuis* was the first Dutch book she'd read since she'd written it, her first thought when she finished was of her childhood friends in Amsterdam, the boys and girls from the Montessori school where she'd learned to read and write. She tried to remember the names of the Christian children, who would have survived the war. She tried to recall the names of her teachers, going all the way back to kindergarten. She pictured the faces of the shopkeepers, the postman, the milk deliveryman who had known her as a child. She imagined their neighbors in the houses on Merwedeplein. And when she had, she saw each of them closing her book and thinking, Who realized she was so gifted? Who realized we had such a writer in our midst?

The first passage she reread was dated over a year before the birth of Amy Bellette. The first time round she'd bent back the corner of the page; the second time, with a pen from her purse, she drew a dark meaningful line in the margin and beside it wrote—in English, of course—"uncanny." (Everything she marked she was marking for him, or made the mark actually pretending to be him.) *I have an odd way of sometimes, as it were, being able to see myself through someone else's eyes. Then I view the affairs of a certain "Anne" at my ease, and browse through the pages of her life as if she were a stranger. Before we came here, when I didn't think about things as much as I do now, I used at times to have the feeling that I didn't belong to Mansa, Pim, and Margot, and that I would always be a bit of an outsider. Sometimes I used to pretend I was an orphan ...*

Then she read the whole thing from the start again, making a small marginal notation—and a small grimace—whenever she came upon anything she was sure he would

168

consider "decorative" or "imprecise" or "unclear." But mostly she marked passages she couldn't believe that she had written as little more than a child. Why, what eloquence, Anne—it gave her gooseflesh, whispering her own name in Boston—what deftness, what wit! How nice, she thought, if I could write like this for Mr. Lonoff's English 12. "It's good," she heard him saying, "it's the best thing you've ever done, Miss Bellette."

But of course it was—she'd had a "great subject," as the girls said in English class. Her family's affinity with what families were suffering everywhere had been clear to her right from the beginning. *There is nothing we can do but wait as calmly as we can till the misery comes to an end. Jews and Christians wait, the whole earth waits; and there are many who wait for death.* But while writing these lines ("Quiet, emphatic feeling—that's the idea. E.I.L.") she had had no grandiose delusions about her little achterhuis diary's ever standing as part of the record of the misery. It wasn't to educate anybody other than herself—out of her great expectations—that she kept track of how trying it all was. Recording it was enduring it; the diary kept her company and it kept her sane, and whenever being her parents' child seemed

169

to her as harrowing as the war itself, it was where she went to confess. Only to Kitty was she able to speak freely about the hopelessness of trying to satisfy her mother the way Margot did; only to Kitty could she openly bewail her inability even to pronounce the word "Mumsie" to her aloud—and to concede the depth of her feeling for Pim, a father she wanted to want her to the exclusion of all others, *not only as his child, but for me— Anne, myself.*

Of course it had eventually to occur to any child so *mad on books and reading* that for all she knew she was writing a book of her own. But most of the time it was her morale that she was sustaining not, at fourteen, literary ambition. As for developing into a writer—she owed that not to any decision to sit down each day and try to be one but to their stifling life. That, of all things, seemed to have nurtured her talent! Truly, without the terror and the claustrophobia of the achterhuis, as a *chatterbox* surrounded by friends and *rollicking with laughter*, free to come and go, free to clown around, free to pursue her every last expectation, would she ever have written sentences so deft and so eloquent and so witty? She thought, Now maybe that's the problem in English 12—not the absence of the great subject but the presence of the lake and the tennis courts and Tanglewood. The perfect tan, the linen skirts, my emerging reputation as the Pallas Athene of Athene College—maybe that's what's doing me in. Maybe if I were locked up again in a room somewhere and fed on rotten potatoes and clothed in rags and terrified out of my wits, maybe then I could write a decent story for Mr. Lonoff!

It was only with the euphoria of *invasion fever*, with the prospect of the Allied landings and the German collapse and the coming of that golden age known around the achterhuis as *after the war*, that she was able to announce to Kitty that the diary had perhaps done more than just assuage her adolescent loneliness. After two years of honing her prose, she felt herself ready for the great undertaking: *my greatest wish is to become a journalist someday and later on a famous writer*. But that was in May of 1944, when to be famous someday seemed to her no more or less extraordinary than to be going back to school in September. Oh, that May of marvelous expectations! Never again another winter in the achterhuis. Another winter and she would have gone crazy.

The first year there it hadn't been that bad;

they'd all been so busy settling in that she didn't have time to feel desperate. In fact, so diligently had they all worked to transform the attic into a *superpractical* home that her father had gotten everybody to agree to subdivide the space still further and take in another Jew. But once the Allied bombing started, the superpractical home became her torture chamber. During the day the two families squabbled over everything, and then at night she couldn't sleep, sure that the Gestapo was going to come in the dark to take them away. In bed she began to have horrifying visions of Lies, her schoolfriend, reproaching her for being safe in bed in Amsterdam and not in a concentration camp, like all her Jewish friends: "*Oh, Anne, why have you deserted me? Help, oh, help me, rescue me from this hell!*" She would see herself *in a dungeon, without Mummy and Daddy*—and worse. Right down to the final hours of 1943 she was dreaming and thinking *the most terrible things*. But then all at once it was over. Miraculously. "And what did it, Professor Lonoff? See *Anna Karenina*. See *Madame Bovary*. See half the literature of the Western world." The miracle: desire. She would be back to school in September, but she would not be returning to class the same girl. She was no longer a girl. Tears would roll down her cheeks at the thought of a naked woman. Her unpleasant menstrual periods became a source of the strangest pleasure. At night in bed she was excited by her breasts. Just these sensations—but all at once forebodings of her miserable death were replaced with a craze for life. One day she was completely recovered, and the next she was, of course, in love. Their troubles had made her her own woman, at fourteen. She began going off on private visits to the secluded corner of the topmost floor, which was occupied exclusively by Peter, the Van Daans' seventeen-year-old son. That she might be stealing him away from Margot didn't stop her, and neither did her scandalized parents: first just teatime visits, then evening assignations—then the defiant letter to the disappointed father. On May 3rd of that marvelous May: *I am young and I possess many buried qualities; I am young and strong and am living a great adventure.* And two days later, to the father who had saved her from the hell that had swallowed up Lies, to the Pim whose favorite living creature she had always longed to be, a declaration of her independence, *in mind and body,* as she bluntly put it: *I have now reached the stage that I can live entirely on my own,*

173

without Mummy's support or anyone else's for that matter . . . I don't feel in the least bit responsible to any of you . . . I don't have to give an account of my deeds to anyone but myself . . .

Well, the strength of a woman on her own wasn't all she'd imagined it to be. Neither was the strength of a loving father. He told her it was the most unpleasant letter he'd ever received, and when she began to cry with shame for having been *too low for words*, he wept along with her. He burned the letter in the fire, the weeks passed, and she found herself growing disenchanted with Peter. In fact, by July she was wondering how it would be possible, in their circumstances, to *shake him off*, a problem resolved for her on a sunny August Friday, when in the middle of the morning, as Pim was helping Peter with his English lessons and she was off studying by herself, the Dutch Green Police arrived and dissolved forever the secret household still heedful of propriety, obedience, discretion, self-improvement, and mutual respect. The Franks, as a family, came to an end, and, fittingly enough, thought the diarist, so did her chronicle of their effort to go sensibly on as themselves, in spite of everything.

The third time she read the book through was on the way back to Stockbridge that evening. Would she ever read another book again? How, if she couldn't put this one down? On the bus she began to speculate in the most immodest way about what she had written— had "wrought." Perhaps what got her going was the rumbling, boundless, electrified, indigo sky that had been stalking the bus down the highway since Boston: outside the window the most outlandish El Greco stage effects, outside a Biblical thunderstorm complete with baroque trimmings, and inside Amy curled up with her book—and with the lingering sense of tragic grandeur she'd soaked up from the real El Grecos that afternoon in the Boston Museum of Fine Arts. And she was exhausted, which probably doesn't hurt fantastical thinking, either. Still spellbound by her first two readings of *Het Achterhuis*, she had rushed on to the Gardner and the Fogg, where, to top off the day, the self-intoxicated girl with the deep tan and the animated walk had been followed by easily a dozen Harvard Summer School students eager to learn her name. Three museums because back at Athene she preferred to tell everyone the truth, more or less, about the

big day in Boston. To Mr. Lonoff she planned
to speak at length about all the new exhibi-
tions she'd gone to see at his wife's suggestion.

The storm, the paintings, her exhaustion—
none of it was really necessary, however, to
inspire the sort of expectations that resulted
from reading her published diary three times
through in the same day. Towering egotism
would probably have been sufficient. Perhaps
she was only a very young writer on a bus
dreaming a very young writer's dreams.

All her reasoning, all her fantastical thinking about the ordained mission of her book
followed from this: neither she nor her parents came through in the diary as anything
like representative of religious or observant
Jews. Her mother lit candles on Friday night
and that was about the extent of it As for
celebrations, she had found St Nicholas's
Day, once she'd been introduced to it in hiding, much more fun than Chanukah, and
along with Pim made all kinds of clever gifts
and even written a Santa Claus poem to en-
liven the festivities When Pim settled upon
a children's Bible as her present for the hol-
iday—so she might learn something about
the New Testament—Margot hadn't ap-

proved. Margot's ambition was to be a midwife in Palestine. She was the only one of them who seemed to have given serious thought to religion. The diary that Margot kept, had it ever been found, would not have been quite so sparing as hers in curiosity about Judaism, or plans for leading a Jewish life. Certainly it was impossible for her to imagine Margot thinking, let alone writing with longing in her diary, *the time will come when we are people again, and not just Jews*

She had written these words, to be sure still suffering the aftereffects of a nighttime burglary in the downstairs warehouse. The burglary had seemed certain to precipitate their discovery by the police, and for days afterward everyone was weak with terror And for her, along with the residue of fear and the dubious sense of relief, there was, of course, the guilt-tinged bafflement when she realized that, unlike Lies, she had again been spared. In the aftermath of that gruesome night, she went around and around trying to understand the meaning of their persecution, one moment writing about the misery of being Jews and only Jews to their enemies, and then in the next airily wondering if *it might even be our religion from which the world and all peoples learn good   We can*

never become just Netherlanders, she reminded Kitty, *we will always remain Jews,
but we want to, too*—only to close out the
argument with an announcement one most
assuredly would not have come upon in "The
Diary of Margot Frank": *I've been saved
again, now my first wish after the war is that
I may become Dutch! I love the Dutch, I love
this country, I love the language and want to
work here. And even if I have to write to the
Queen myself, I will not give up until I have
reached my goal.*

No, that wasn't mother's Margot talking,
that was father's Anne. To London to learn
English, to Paris to look at clothes and study
art, to Hollywood, California, to interview
the stars as someone named "Anne Frank-
lin"—while self-sacrificing Margot delivered
babies in the desert. To be truthful, while
Margot was thinking about God and the
homeland, the only deities she ever seemed
to contemplate at any length were to be found
in the mythology of Greece and Rome, which
she studied all the time in hiding, and adored.
To be truthful, the young girl of her diary
was, compared to Margot, only dimly Jewish,
though in that entirely the daughter of the
father who calmed her fears by reading aloud

to her at night not the Bible but Goethe in German and Dickens in English.

But that was the point—that was what gave her diary the power to make the nightmare real. To expect the great callous and indifferent world to care about the child of a pious, bearded father living under the sway of the rabbis and the rituals—that was pure folly. To the ordinary person with no great gift for tolerating even the smallest of differences the plight of that family wouldn't mean a thing. To ordinary people it probably would seem that they had invited disaster by stubbornly repudiating everything modern and European—not to say Christian. But the family of Otto Frank, that would be another matter! How could even the most obtuse of the ordinary ignore what had been done to the Jews *just for being Jews*, how could even the most benighted of the Gentiles fail to get the idea when they read in *Het Achterhuis* that once a year the Franks sang a harmless Chanukah song, said some Hebrew words, lighted some candles, exchanged some presents—a ceremony lasting about ten minutes—and that was all it took to make them the enemy. It did not even take that much. It took nothing that was the horror And that was the truth. And that was the power of her book. The Franks could gather together by the radio to listen to concerts of Mozart, Brahms, and Beethoven; they could entertain themselves with Goethe and Dickens and Schiller; she could look night after night through the genealogical tables of all of Europe's royal families for suitable mates for Princess Elizabeth and Princess Margaret Rose; she could write passionately in her diary of her love for Queen Wilhelmina and her desire for Holland to be her fatherland—and none of it made any difference. Europe was not theirs nor were they Europe's, not even her Europeanized family. Instead, three flights up from a pretty Amsterdam canal, they lived crammed into a hundred square feet with the Van Daans, as isolated and despised as any ghetto Jews. First expulsion, next confinement, and then, in cattle cars and camps and ovens, obliteration. And why? Because the Jewish problem to be solved, the degenerates whose contamination civilized people could no longer abide, were they themselves, Otto and Edith Frank, and their daughters, Margot and Anne.

This was the lesson that on the journey home she came to believe she had the power to teach. But only if she were believed to be dead. Were *Het Achterhuis* known to be the work of a living writer, it would never be more than it was: a young teenager's diary of her trying years in hiding during the German occupation of Holland, something boys and girls could read in bed at night along with the adventures of the Swiss Family Robinson. But dead she had something more to offer than amusement for ages 10–15; dead she had written, without meaning to or trying to, a book with the force of a masterpiece to make people finally see.

And when people had finally seen? When they had learned what she had the power to teach them, what then? Would suffering come to mean something new to them? Could she actually make them humane creatures for any longer than the few hours it would take to read her diary through? In her room at Athene—after hiding in her dresser the three copies of *Het Achterhuis*—she thought more calmly about her readers-to-be than she had while pretending to be one of them on the stirring bus ride through the lightning storm. She was not, after all, the fifteen-year-old who could, while hiding from a holocaust, tell Kitty, *I still believe that people are really good at heart.* Her youthful ideals had suffered no less than she had in the windowless freight car from Westerbork and in the barracks at Auschwitz and on the Belsen heath. She had not come to hate the human race for what it was—what could it be but what it was?—but she did not feel seemly any more singing its praises.

What would happen when people had finally seen? The only realistic answer was Nothing. To believe anything else was only to yield to longings which even she, the great longer, had a right to question by now. To keep her existence a secret from her father so as to help improve mankind . . . no, not at this late date. The improvement of the living was their business, not hers; they could improve themselves, if they should ever be so disposed; and if not, not. Her responsibility was to the dead, if to anyone—to her sister, to her mother, to all the slaughtered school-children who had been her friends. There was her diary's purpose, there was her ordained mission: to restore in print their status as flesh and blood . . . for all the good that would do them. An ax was what she really wanted, not print. On the stairwell at the end of her corridor in the dormitory there was a large ax with an enormous red handle, to be used in case of fire. But what about in case of hatred—what about murderous rage? She stared at it often enough, but never found the nerve to take it down from the wall. Besides, once she had it in her hands, whose head would she split open? Whom could she kill in Stockbridge to avenge the ashes and the skulls? If she even could wield it. No, what she had been given to wield was *Het Achterhuis, van Anne Frank.* And to draw blood with it she would have to vanish again into another achterhuis, this time fatherless and all on her own.

So she renewed her belief in the power of her less than three hundred pages, and with it the resolve to keep from her father, sixty, the secret of her survival. "For them," she cried, "for them," meaning all who had met the fate that she had been spared and was now pretending to. "For Margot, for my mother, for Lies."

Now every day she went to the library to read *The New York Times.* Each week she read carefully through the newsmagazines. On Sundays she read about all the new books being published in America: novels said to be "notable" and "significant," none of which could possibly be more notable and more significant than her posthumously published diary; insipid best-sellers from which real people learned about fake people who could not exist and would not matter if they did. She read praise for historians and biographers whose books, whatever their merit, couldn't possibly be as worthy of recognition as hers. And in every column in every periodical she found in the library—American, French, German, English—she looked for her own real name. It could not end with just a few thousand Dutch readers shaking their heads and going about their business—it was too important for that! "For them, for them"—over and over, week after week, "for them"—until at last she began to wonder if having survived in the achterhuis, if having outlived the death camps, if masquerading here in New England as somebody other than herself did not make something very suspect—and a little mad—of this seething passion to "come back" as the avenging ghost. She began to fear that she was succumbing to having not succumbed.

And why should she! Who was she pretending to be but who she would have been anyway if no achterhuis and no death camps had intervened? Amy was not somebody else. The Amy who had rescued her from her memories and restored her to life—beguiling, commonsensical, brave, and realistic Amy—was herself. Who she had every right to be! Responsibility to the dead? Rhetoric for the pious! There was nothing to give the dead—they were dead. "Exactly. The importance, so-called, of this book is a morbid illusion. And playing dead is melodramatic and disgusting. And hiding from Daddy is worse. No atonement is required," said Amy to Anne. "Just get on the phone and tell Pim you're alive. He is sixty."

Her longing for him now exceeded even what it had been in childhood, when she wanted more than anything to be his only love. But she was young and strong and she was living a great adventure, and she did nothing to inform him or anyone that she was still alive; and then one day it was just too late. No one would have believed her; no one other than her father would have wanted to. Now people came every day to visit their secret hideaway and to look at the photographs of the movie stars that she'd pinned to the wall beside her bed. They came to see the tub she had bathed in and the table where she'd studied. They looked out of the loft window where Peter and she had cuddled together watching the stars. They stared at the cupboard camouflaging the door the police had come through to take them away. They looked at the open pages of her secret diary.

That was her handwriting, they whispered, those are her words. They stayed to look at everything in the achterhuis that she had ever touched. The plain passageways and serviceable little rooms that she had, like a good composition student, dutifully laid out for Kitty in orderly, accurate, workaday Dutch— the superpractical achterhuis was now a holy shrine, a Wailing Wall. They went away from it in silence, as bereft as though she had been their own.

But it was they who were hers. "They wept for me," said Amy; "they pitied me; they prayed for me; they begged my forgiveness. I was the incarnation of the millions of un-lived years robbed from the murdered Jews. It was too late to be alive now. I was a saint."

That was her story. And what did Lonoff think of it when she was finished? That she meant every word and that not a word was true.

After Amy had showered and dressed, she checked out of the hotel and he took her to eat some lunch. He phoned Hope from the restaurant and explained that he was bringing Amy home. She could walk in the woods, look at the foliage, sleep safely in Becky's bed; over a few days' time she would be able to collect herself, and then she could return

186

to Cambridge. All he explained about her collapse was that she appeared to him to be suffering from exhaustion. He had promised Amy that he would say no more.

On the ride back to the Berkshires, while Amy told him what it had been like for her during the years when she was being read in twenty different languages by twenty million people, he made plans to consult Dr. Boyce. Boyce was at Riggs, the Stockbridge psychiatric hospital. Whenever a new book appeared, Dr. Boyce would send a charming note asking the author if he would kindly sign the doctor's copy, and once a year the Lonoffs were invited to the Boyces' big barbecue. At Dr. Boyce's request, Lonoff once reluctantly consented to meet with a staff study group from the hospital to discuss "the creative personality." He didn't want to offend the psychiatrist, and it might for a while pacify his wife, who liked to believe that if he got out and mixed more with people things would be better at home.

The study group turned out to have ideas about writing that were too imaginative for his taste, but he made no effort to tell them they were wrong. Nor did he think that he was necessarily right. They saw it their way, he saw it like Lonoff. Period. He had no desire to change anyone's mind. Fiction made people say all kinds of strange things—so be it.

The meeting with the psychiatrists had been underway for only an hour when Lonoff said it had been an enjoyable evening but he had to be getting home. "I have the evening's reading still ahead of me. Without my reading I'm not myself. However, you must feel free to talk about my personality when I'm gone." Boyce, smiling warmly, replied, "I hope we've amused you at least a little with our naïve speculations." "I would have liked to amuse *you*. I apologize for being boring." "No, no," said Boyce, "passivity in a man of stature has a charm and mystery all its own." "Yes?" said Lonoff. "I must tell my wife."

But an hour wasted some five years ago was hardly to the point. He trusted Boyce and knew that the psychiatrist would not betray his confidence when he went the next day to talk with him about his former student and quasi daughter, a young woman of twenty-six, who had disclosed to him that of all the Jewish writers, from Franz Kafka to E. I. Lonoff, she was the most famous. As for his own betrayal of the quasi daughter's confidence, it did not count for much as Amy elaborated further upon her consuming delusion.

"Do you know why I took this sweet name?

It wasn't to protect me from my memories. I wasn't hiding the past from myself or myself from the past. I was hiding from hatred, from hating people the way people hate spiders and rats. Manny, I felt flayed. I felt as though the skin had been peeled away from half my body. Half my face had been peeled away, and everybody would stare in horror for the rest of my life. Or they would stare at the other half, at the half still intact; I could see them smiling, pretending that the flayed half wasn't there, and talking to the half that was. And I could hear myself screaming at them, I could see myself thrusting my hideous side right up into their unmarred faces to make them properly horrified. 'I was pretty! I was whole! I was a sunny, lively little girl! Look, look at what they did to me!' But whatever side they looked at, I would always be screaming, 'Look at the other! Why don't you look at the other!' That's what I thought about in the hospital at night. However they look at me, however they talk to me, however they try to comfort me, I will always be this half-flayed thing. I will never be young, I will never be kind or at peace or in love, and I will hate them all my life.

"So I took the sweet name—to impersonate everything that I wasn't. And a very good

pretender I was, too. After a while I could
imagine that I wasn't pretending at all, that
I had become what I would have been anyway. Until the book. The package came from
Amsterdam, I opened it, and there it was: my
past, myself, my name, *my face intact*—and
all I wanted was revenge. It wasn't for the
dead—it had nothing to do with bringing
back the dead or scourging the living. It
wasn't corpses I was avenging—it was the
motherless, fatherless, sisterless, venge-filled,
hate-filled, shame-filled, half-flayed, seething thing. It was myself. I wanted tears, I
wanted their Christian tears to run like Jewish blood, for me. I wanted their pity—and
in the most pitiless way. And I wanted love,
to be loved mercilessly and endlessly, just the
way I'd been debased. I wanted my fresh life
and my fresh body, cleansed and unpolluted.
And it needed twenty million people for that.
Twenty million ten times over.

"Oh, Manny, I want to live with you! That's
what I need! The millions won't do it—it's
you! I want to go home to Europe with you.
Listen to me, don't say no, not yet. This summer I saw a small house for rent, a stone villa
up on a hillside. It was outside Florence. It
had a pink tile roof and a garden. I got the
phone number and I wrote it down. I still

190

have it. Oh, everything beautiful that I saw in Italy made me think of how happy you could be there—how happy I would be there, looking after you. I thought of the trips we'd take. I thought of the afternoons in the museums and having coffee later by the river. I thought of listening to music together at night. I thought of making your meals. I thought of wearing lovely nightgowns to bed. Oh, Manny, their Anne Frank is theirs; I want to be *your* Anne Frank. I'd like at last to be my own. Child Martyr and Holy Saint isn't a position I'm really qualified for any more. They wouldn't even have me, not as I am, longing for somebody else's husband, begging him to leave his loyal wife to run off with a girl half his age. Manny, does it matter that I'm your daughter's age and you're my father's? Of course I love the Dad-da in you, how could I not? And if you love the child in me, why shouldn't you? There's nothing strange in that—so does half the world. Love has to start somewhere, and that's where it starts in us. And as for who I am—well," said Amy, in a voice as sweet and winning as any he'd ever heard, "you've got to be somebody, don't you? There's no way around that."

At home they put her to bed. In the kitchen Lonoff sat with his wife drinking the coffee she'd made him. Every time he pictured Amy at the dentist's office reading about Otto Frank in *Time* magazine, or in the library stacks searching for her "real" name, every time he imagined her on Boston Common addressing to her writing teacher an intimate disquisition on "her" book, he wanted to let go and cry. He had never suffered so over the suffering of another human being.

Of course he told Hope nothing about who Amy thought she was. But he didn't have to, he could guess what she would say if he did: it was for him, the great writer, that Amy had chosen to become Anne Frank; that explained it all, no psychiatrist required. For him, as a consequence of her infatuation: to enchant him, to bewitch him, to break through the scrupulosity and the wisdom and the virtue into his imagination, and there, as Anne Frank, to become E I Lonoff's *femme fatale*

4

Married to Tolstoy

The next morning we all ate breakfast together like a happy family of four. The woman whom Lonoff could not throw out after thirty years just because he might prefer to see a new face over his fruit juice proudly told us—over our fruit juice—of the accomplishments of the children whose chairs Amy and I occupied. She showed us recent photographs of them, all with their own children. Lonoff had not mentioned to me the night before that he was a grandfather several times over. But why would he?

Hope seemed overnight to have been transformed from his aging, aggrieved, lonely wife into somebody rather more like the happy author of the sweet nature poems framed on the kitchen wall, the tender of the geraniums, the woman of whom Lonoff had said over the broken saucer, "She can glue it." Nor did Lonoff seem quite the same man; whether deliberately or not, he was humming "My Blue Heaven" when he came to the breakfast table. And almost immediately began the mordant clowning, also designed to make Hope all the happier.

And why the change? Because Amy would return to Cambridge after breakfast.

But I could not really think of her as Amy any longer. Instead I was continually drawn back into the fiction I had evolved about her and the Lonoffs while I lay in the dark study, transported by his praise and throbbing with resentment of my disapproving father—and, of course, overcome by what had passed between my idol and the marvelous young woman before he had manfully gone back to bed with his wife.

Throughout breakfast, my father, my mother, the judge and Mrs. Wapter were never out of my thoughts. I'd gone the whole night without sleep, and now I couldn't think straight about them or myself, or about Amy, as she was called. I kept seeing myself coming back to New Jersey and saying to my family, "I met a marvelous young woman while I was up in New England. I love her and she loves me. We are going to be married." "Married? But so fast? Nathan, is she Jewish?" "Yes, she is." "But who is she?" "Anne Frank."

"I eat too much," said Lonoff, as Hope poured the water for his tea.

"It's exercise you need," Hope said. "It's more walking. You gave up your afternoon walk and so you began to gain weight. You actually eat almost nothing. Certainly nothing that's fattening. It's sitting at the desk that does it. And staying in the house."

"I can't face another walk. I can't face those trees again."

"Then walk in the other direction."

"For ten years I walked in the other direction. That's why I started walking in this direction. Besides, I'm not even walking when I'm walking. The truth is, I don't even see the trees."

"That's not so," Hope said. "He loves nature," she informed me. "He knows the name of everything that grows."

"I'm cutting down on my food," said Lonoff. "Who wants to split an egg with me?"

Hope said, happily, "You can treat yourself to a whole egg this morning."

"Amy, you want to split an egg with me?"

His invitation for her to speak gave me my first opportunity to turn her way without embarrassment. It was so. It *could* be. The same look of unarmored and unimpaired intelligence, the same musing look of serene anticipation . . . The forehead wasn't Shakespeare's—it was *hers*.

She was smiling, as though she too were in the best of spirits and his refusal to kiss her breasts the night before had never happened. "Couldn't do it," she said to him.

"Not even half?" asked Lonoff.

"Not even a sixteenth."

This is my Aunt Tessie, this is Frieda and Dave, this is Birdie, this is Murray . . . as you see, we are an enormous family. This is my wife, everyone. She is all I have ever wanted. If you doubt me, just look at her smile, listen to her laugh. Remember the shadowed eyes innocently uplifted in the clever little face? Remember the dark hair clipped back with a barrette? Well, this is she. . . . Anne, says my father—the Anne? *Oh, how I have misunderstood my son. How mistaken we have been!*

"Scramble an egg, Hope," said Lonoff. "I'll eat half if you'll eat half."

196

"You can eat the whole thing," she replied. "Just start taking your walks again."

He looked at me, imploringly. "Nathan, eat half."

"No, no," said his wife and, turning to the stove, announced triumphantly, "You'll eat the whole egg!"

Beaten, Lonoff said, "And to top things off, I threw out my razor blade this morning."

"And why," said Amy, pretending still to be in her blue heaven too, "did you do a thing like that?"

"I thought it through. My children are finished with college. My house is paid for. I have Blue Cross and Major Medical protection. I have a '56 Ford. Yesterday I got a check for forty-five dollars in royalties from Brazil—money out of the blue. Throw it out, I told myself, and have a fresh shave with a new blade. Then I thought: No, there's at least one shave left in this blade, maybe even two. Why be wasteful? But then I thought it through further: I have seven books on the paperback racks, I have publishers in twenty countries, there's a new shingle roof on the house; there's a quiet furnace in the basement, there's brand-new plumbing in Hope's little bathroom. The bills are all paid, and what is more, there is money left over in the bank that is earning three percent interest for our old age. The hell with it, I thought, enough thinking—and I put in a new blade. And look how I butchered myself. I almost took my ear off."

Amy: "Proves you shouldn't be impulsive."

"I only wanted to see what it was like living like everybody else."

"And?" asked Hope, back at the table now, frying pan in hand.

"I told you. I almost took my ear off."

"Here's your egg."

"I only want half."

"Darling, feast for once," said Hope, kissing his head.

Dear Mom and Dad: We have been with Anne's father for three days now. They have both been in the most moving state of exaltation since our arrival . . .

"And here's your mail," said Hope.

"I never used to look at this stuff until the end of the day," he explained to me.

"He wouldn't even look at the newspaper headlines," said Hope. "He wouldn't even eat breakfast with us until a few years ago. But when the children were all gone, I refused to sit here by myself."

"But I wouldn't let you talk to me, would I? That's new."

"Let me make you another egg," she said.

He pushed aside his empty plate. "No, darling, no. I'm full."

Dear Folks: Anne is pregnant, and happier, she says, than she ever thought possible again...

He was sorting now through the half dozen letters in his hand. He said to me, "This is what gets forwarded from a publisher. One in a hundred is worth opening. In five hundred."

"What about a secretary to open them?" I asked.

"He's too conscientious," Hope explained. "He can't do it that way. Besides, a secretary is another person. We can't turn the house into Grand Central Station."

"A secretary is six other people," he informed her.

"What is it this time?" she asked Lonoff as he turned over the penciled sheets in his hand. "Read it, Manny."

"You read it." He handed the letter across to his wife. "Let Nathan see what it is to be lifted from obscurity. Let him not come hammering at our door to tell us that he wasn't warned."

She wiped her hands on her apron and took the letter. It was quite a morning she was

199

having, a new life altogether. And why? Because Amy was on her way.

"'Dear Mr. Lonoff,'" she read. "'I suggest that you with your talent write a story with the following plot. A non-Jew comes from the West to New York City and meets Jews for the first time. Being a good-natured person he does them favors. When he gives up part of his lunch hour at work to help them, they act like pigs in getting as much of his time as possible. When he helps his co-workers by getting them ball-point pens wholesale, the same happens. They try to get him to buy some for strangers by saying, "A man I know wants to buy a dozen pens," and saying later, "I didn't tell you to, I didn't ask you to buy them for him, I only told you I wanted two dozen and you can't tell me I told you to buy him two dozen." Consequently he develops a dislike for Jews. Later he finds out that non-Jews who don't try to impose are trying to put him out of a job while the Jews take his side when the boss wants to fire him. When he gets sick, the Jews donate blood for him. At the end he has a conversation with a person in which he learns how the history of the Jews led to their habit of opportunism. Yours truly, Ray W. Oliver. P.S. I am also a writer of short stories. I am willing to collaborate with you on a story using that plot.'"

"Me too," said Amy.

"The consequences of his infatuation," I said. A line out of "The Middle Years," but not even Lonoff seemed to remember it. "From Henry James," I added, flushing. "'The rest is the madness of art.'"

"Aha," said Lonoff.

Ass! Idiot! I had been caught—while showing off my erudition!

Aha. He knew everything.

But rather than asking me to get up and go because of the way I had behaved in his study, he opened a second letter and removed the small index card inside. He read it and handed it to Hope.

"Oh, these," she said. "They make me so angry."

"Has style, however," said Lonoff. "I like the absence of the salutation. Just puts out the line and hangs up the wash. Read it, Hopie."

"I hate these, so."

"Go on. For Nathan's edification."

Then he *didn't* know. Or knew and forgave me.

"'I have just finished your brilliant story, "Indiana,"'" Hope read. "'What do you know about the Middle West, you little Jewish shit? Your Jew omniscience is about as agreeable to the average person as is your kike sense of "art." Sally M., Fort Wayne.'"

Lonoff, meanwhile, had been carefully slicing open a blue overseas air letter.

"New Delhi," he announced.

"You've been made a Brahman," said Amy.

Hope smiled at the girl who would be gone now in less than an hour. "He won't accept."

"Well," replied Amy, "maybe he's in luck and they made him an Untouchable."

"Or less," said Lonoff, and handed the letter to Hope.

"You can't have everything," Amy told him.

Hope read, this time without being prompted. "'Dear Sir, I am a twenty-two-year-old youth from India. I introduce myself as there is no other way to make your acquaintance. Perhaps you may not relish the idea of being acquainted with a stranger who is bent on exploiting you.'" Here, suddenly, her confidence seemed shaken, and she looked up at Lonoff, confused as to what to do next.

He told her. "Go on."

"—'bent on exploiting you. I beg your assistance fully aware of the barriers like caste, creed, etc., that divide us. As I am just a beggar in different garb I will put forward my request rather impetuously. My desire is to settle down in America. Will you please take me out of my country by some means? If my educational qualification disqualifies me from entering America as a student, and if all other means fail, will you just adopt me as the last resort? I am quite ashamed to write such a request for I am so old and I have parents who depend upon me to provide for them during their old age. I shall do any kind of work and I will try my best to be of some use to you. Sir, by now you would have formed in your mind the unimpressive figure of a short, dark, ambitious Indian guy whose character is sprinkled with a generous amount of jealousy. If you have thought in the above manner you are in for a surprise. For the above description suits me to the core. I want to escape from the harsh realities and live with some peace and pursue part-time education. Sir, please let me know whether it is possible for you to assist your humble servant—'"

Hope brought the letter to her chest—she

saw that Amy had pushed back her chair and was standing. "I'm sorry," Hope said to her.

"Why?" asked Amy, forcing a smile.

Hope's hands began to tremble.

I glanced toward Lonoff, but he was saying nothing.

With just a tinge of exasperation, Amy said, "I don't understand why you should be sorry."

Hope undertook to fold the letter from India, though not with any method I could discern. Her eyes went to the geraniums when she said, "I didn't mean to embarrass you."

"But I'm not embarrassed," said Amy, innocently.

"I didn't *say* you were," Hope conceded. "I said I didn't *mean* to."

Amy didn't follow—that was the act. She waited for Hope to explain herself further.

"Forget it, please," said Hope.

"It's forgotten," Lonoff said softly.

"I'm going now," Amy said to him.

"Must you," asked Lonoff, "without finishing the coffee?"

"You're half an hour behind schedule already," Amy said. "What with all this promiscuous socializing over your egg, it could take you the rest of the morning to recover."

"Yes," I said, jumping up, "and I have to be off, too."

"There's no bus this early," Lonoff informed me. "The first bus north arrives at eleven-twenty."

"Still, if she could drop me in town, I'll just walk around—if that's not out of your way," I added, and looked as shyly as I had the day before at the girl I had veiled in so many imaginings, and whom *still* I couldn't see plain.

"Suit yourself," said Lonoff.

He rose and came around the table to kiss Amy on her cheek. "Stay in touch," he told her. "And thanks for the help."

"I think I at least got each of the books separated out. At least that's in order."

"Fine. The rest I have to see to myself. And think about. I'm not sure it's for me, my friend."

"Please," she said, "I beseech you, don't destroy anything."

A charade it may have been, but still I understood her to be entreating him about the worksheets of his old stories that she had been sorting for the Harvard manuscript collection. But to Hope the girl's request clearly had a less innocent intention. Before either of them could speak another double entendre in her presence, Hope was out of the room.

We heard her mount the stairs, and then the bedroom door slammed shut overhead.

"Excuse me one moment," said Lonoff, and buttoning his jacket, he followed after his wife.

Silently Amy and I took our things from the hall closet and got dressed for the snow. Then we stood there trying to decide what to do next. I had all I could do not to say, "Did you ever have the feeling that you wanted to go, still have the feeling that you wanted to stay?"

What I came up with was not much better "Last night at dinner he told me about the letter that you sent him from England."

She took this in and went back to waiting. On her head was the white wool cap with the long tassel that ended in a fluffy white ball. Of course! He had given it to her, her first winter here in the Berkshires; and now she could not part with it, no more than she could part with him, her second Pim.

"When was that?" I asked. "When were you living in England?"

"Oh, my." She closed her eyes and pressed one hand to her forehead. I saw then how very tired she was. Neither of us had slept the night before, she thinking of who she might become living in Florence with Lonoff, and I thinking of who she might have been. When the sleeve of her coat fell back, I of course saw that there was no scar on her forearm. No scar; no book; no Pim. No, the loving father who must be relinquished for the sake of his child's art was not hers; he was mine. "I was short, dark, ambitious—and sixteen. Eleven years ago," she said.

Making her Anne Frank's age exactly, had she survived.

"Where had you been before England?"

"That's a long story."

"You'd been through the war?"

"I missed the war."

"How so?"

She smiled politely. I was getting on her nerves. "Luck."

"I suppose that's how I missed it too," I replied.

"And what did you have instead?" she asked me.

"My childhood. What did *you* have instead?"

Dryly she said, "Somebody else's. I think perhaps we should go, Mr. Zuckerman. I have to be off. It's a long drive."

"I'd rather not leave without saying good-bye."

"I'd rather not, either, but we better."

"I'm sure he wanted us to wait."

"Oh, did he?" she said strangely, and I followed her into the living room, where we sat in the easy chairs beside the fireplace. She had taken Lonoff's chair and I took my place in the other. Angrily she removed the hat.

"He's been awfully generous to me," I explained. "It's been quite a visit. For me," I added.

"He's a generous man."

"He helped you to come to America."

"Yes."

"From England."

She picked up the magazine that I'd leafed through the evening before while Lonoff spoke on the phone.

I said, "Pardon me, for insisting..."

She smiled vaguely at me and began turning pages.

"It's just—that you bear some resemblance to Anne Frank."

A shiver went down my body when she replied, "I've been told that before."

"You *have?*"

"But," she said, bringing her intelligent

eyes directly up to mine, "I'm afraid I'm not she."

Silence.

"You've read her book, however."

"Not really," she said. "I looked at it "

"Oh, but it's quite a book."

"Is it?"

"Oh, yes. She was a marvelous young writer. She was something for thirteen It's like watching an accelerated film of a fetus sprouting a face, watching her mastering things. You must read it. Suddenly she's discovering reflection, suddenly there's portraiture, character sketches, suddenly there's a long intricate eventful happening so beautifully recounted it seems to have gone through a dozen drafts. And no poisonous notion of being *interesting* or *serious*. She just *is*." My whole body was damp from the effort of compressing my thoughts and presenting them to her before Lonoff returned to inhibit me "The ardor in her, the spirit in her—always on the move, always starting things, being boring as unbearable to her as being bored— a terrific writer, really. And an enormously appealing child. I was thinking"—the thought had only just occurred to me, of course, in the rapture of praising Anne Frank to one who might even be her—"she's like some impassioned little sister of Kafka's, his lost little daughter—a kinship is even there in the face. I think. Kafka's garrets and closets, the hidden attics where they hand down the indictments, the camouflaged doors—everything he dreamed in Prague was, to her, real Amsterdam life. What he invented, she suffered. Do you remember the first sentence of *The Trial*? We were talking about it last night, Mr. Lonoff and myself. It could be the epigraph for her book. 'Someone must have falsely traduced Anne F., because one morning without having done anything wrong, she was placed under arrest.'"

However, despite *my* ardor, Amy's mind was elsewhere. But then so was mine, really—back in New Jersey, where the lucky childhood had been spent. To be wed somehow to you, I thought, my unassailable advocate, my invulnerable ally, my shield against their charges of defection and betrayal and reckless, heinous informing! Oh, marry me, Anne Frank, exonerate me before my outraged elders of this idiotic indictment! Heedless of Jewish feeling? Indifferent to Jewish survival? Brutish about their well-being? Who dares to accuse of such unthinking crimes the husband of Anne Frank!

But, alas, I could not lift her out of her sacred book and make her a character in this life. Instead, I was confronted by Amy Bellette (whoever *she* might be), turning the pages of Lonoff's magazine, and, while she savored his every underlining, waiting to see if at the last minute he would not change his life, and hers with it. The rest was so much fiction, the unchallengeable answer to their questionnaire that I proposed to offer the Wapters. And far from being unchallengeable, far from acquitting me of their charges and restoring to me my cherished blamelessness, a fiction that of course would seem to them a desecration even more vile than the one they had read.

Hope was coming down the stairs, dressed for the outdoors in a hooded green loden coat and wearing snow boots pulled over her wool trousers. She held firmly to the banister with one hand—to prevent herself from falling—and in the other carried a small overnight bag.

Lonoff spoke to her from the top of the stairs. "This won't do," he said softly. "This is pure—"

"Let's all have what we want, please." She spoke without looking back at him; in her emotional state she had all she could do to negotiate the stairs.

"This is hardly what you want."

She stopped—"It is what I have wanted for *years*"—then proceeded once more with leaving home.

"Come back up here. You don't know what you're saying."

"You're just frightened," she said, from between her teeth, "of losing your boredom."

"I can't hear you, Hope."

Safely now at the bottom landing, the little woman turned and looked up the stairs. "You're just worried about how you will get all your writing done and all your reading done and all your brooding done without the boredom of me. Well, let someone else be boring for you from now on! Let someone else be no trouble!"

"Please come back up here."

Rather than doing as he asked, she picked up her bag and came into the living room. I alone stood to receive her.

"Take off your coat," she said to Amy. "Now *you're* going to have thirty-five years of it!" And with that she began to shake with sobs.

Lonoff was now making the cautious trek down the stairs. "Hope, this is playacting. And pure indulgence."

"I am going," she told him.

"You're not going anywhere. Put the bag down."

"No! I am going to Boston! But don't worry—she knows where everything is. It's practically home to her already. No precious time will be lost. She can hang her things back in the closet and be ready to begin boring you as soon as I'm out the door. You won't even notice the difference."

Amy, unable to watch any longer, looked down into her lap, prompting Hope to say, "Oh, she thinks otherwise. Of course she does. I've seen her fondling each sheet of each draft of each story. She thinks with her it will all be the religion of art up here. Oh, will it ever! Let her try to please you, Manny! Let her serve as the backdrop for your thoughts for thirty-five years. Let her see how noble and heroic you are by the twenty-seventh draft. Let her cook you wonderful meals and light candles for your dinner. Let her get everything ready to make you happy and then see the look on your stone face when you come in at night and sit down at the table. A surprise for dinner? Oh, my dear girl, that is merely his due for a miserable day of bad writing. *That* gets no rise out of him. And candles in the old pewter holders? Candles,

213

after all these years? How poignant of her, he thinks, how vulgar, what a wistful souvenir of yesterday's tearooms. Yes, have her run hot baths for your poor back twice a day, and then go a week without being talked to— let alone being touched in bed. Ask him in bed, 'What is it, dear, what's the matter?' But of course you know all too well what the matter is—you know why he won't hold you, why he doesn't even know you're *there*. The fiftieth draft!"

"That is enough," said Lonoff. "Quite thorough, very accurate, and enough."

"Fondling those papers of yours! Oh, she'll see! I got fondled more by strangers on the rush-hour subway during two months in 1935 than I have up here in the last twenty years! Take off your coat, Amy—you're staying. The classroom daydream has come true! You get the creative writer—and I get to go!"

"She's not staying," Lonoff said, softly again. "You're staying."

"Not for thirty-five more years of this!"

"Oh, Hopie." He put a hand out to her face, where the tears were still falling.

"I'm going to Boston! I'm going to Europe! It's too late to touch me now! I'm taking a trip around the world and never coming back! And you," she said, looking down at Amy in her chair, "*you* won't go anywhere. *You* won't see anything. If you even go out to dinner, if once in six months you get him to accept an invitation to somebody's home, then it'll be even worse—then for the hour before you go your life will be misery from his kvetching about what it's going to be like when those people start in with their *ideas*. If you dare to change the *pepper* mill, he'll ask what's the matter, what was wrong with the old one? It takes three months for him just to get used to a new brand of *soap*. Change the soap and he goes around the house *sniffing*, as though something dead is on the bathroom sink instead of just a bar of Palmolive. Nothing can be touched, nothing can be changed, everybody must be quiet, the children must shut up, their friends must stay away until four— There is his religion of art, my young successor: rejecting life! *Not* living is what he makes his beautiful fiction *out* of! And you will now be the person he is not living with!"

Amy pushed herself up out of her chair and put on the childish hat with the ball on the end of the tassel. Looking past Hope, she said to Lonoff, "I'm going."

"*I'm* going," Hope cried.

To me Amy said, "I'm leaving now, if you'd like a ride to town."

"*I'm* leaving now," Hope told her. "Take that silly hat off! School is over! You are twenty-seven! This is officially your house!"

"It's not, Hope," Amy said, beginning at last to cry. "It's yours."

And so broken and pathetic did she seem in that moment of capitulation that I thought, But of course last night is not the first time she's sat cuddled up in his lap—but of course he's seen her unclothed before. They have been lovers! Yet when I tried to imagine E. I. Lonoff stripped of his suit and on his back, and Amy naked and astride his belly, I couldn't, no more than any son can.

I don't think I could keep my wits about me, teaching such beautiful and gifted and fetching girls.

Then you shouldn't do it.

Oh, Father, is this so, were you the lover of this lovesick, worshipful, displaced daughter half your age? Knowing full well you'd never leave Hope? You succumbed too? Can that be? *You?*

The bed? I had the bed.

Convinced now that that wasn't so—that nobody, nobody, has ever really *had* the bed—I persisted nonetheless in believing that it was.

"You do as I say!" Hope again, ordering

Amy. "You stay and look after him! He cannot stay here alone!"

"But I won't be alone," Lonoff explained to her. "You know that I won't be alone. Enough, enough now, for your sake, too. This is all because we've had visitors. This is all because somebody new stayed the night. There was company, we all had breakfast, and you got excited. Now everybody's going away—and this came over you. You got lonely. You got frightened. Everybody understands."

"Look, Manny, *she* is the child—don't you treat *me* like the child! She is now the child-bride here—"

But before Hope could describe her in further detail, Amy was past her and out the front door.

"Oh, the little bitch!" cried Hope.

"Hope," said Lonoff. "Don't. Not that routine."

But he did not move to stop her as she too ran from the house, carrying her bag.

I said, "Do you want me—to do anything?"

"No, no. Let it run its course."

"Okay."

"Calm down, Nathan. One at a time we are about to calm down."

Then we heard Hope scream.

I followed him to the front window, expecting to see blood on the snow. Instead, there was Hope, seated in a drift only a few feet from the house, while Amy's car was slowly backing out of the car shed. But for the billowing exhaust fumes everything out of doors was gleaming. It was as though not one but two suns had risen that morning.

Hope watched, we watched. The car turned in the driveway. Then it was out onto the road and gone.

"Mrs. Lonoff's fallen down."

"I see that," he said sadly.

We watched her struggle to her feet. Lonoff rapped on the frosted window with his knuckles. Without bothering to look back up to the house, Hope retrieved the overnight bag from where it lay on the path and proceeded with cautious tiny steps to the car shed, where she got into the Lonoffs' Ford. But the car only whined when she tried to start it; effort after effort produced only the most disheartening of winter sounds.

"The battery," he explained.

"Maybe she flooded it."

Again she tried: same results.

"No, the battery," he said. "It's been happening all month. You charge it up and it makes no difference."

"You may need a new one," I said, since that was what he wanted to talk about.

"I shouldn't. The car is practically brand-new. Where does it go but into town?"

We waited, and finally Hope got out of the car.

"Well, good thing you got a lemon," I said.

"Perhaps." He walked around to the hallway and opened the front door. I continued to watch from the window.

"Hope," he called. "Come in now. That's it."

"No!"

"But how can I live alone?"

"The boy can live with you."

"Don't be silly. The boy is going. Come inside now. If you slip again, you're going to get hurt. Darling, it's slippery, it's cold as hell—"

"I'm going to Boston."

"How will you do that?"

"I'll walk if I have to."

"Hope, it's twenty degrees. Come back in and get warm and calm down. Have some tea with me. Then we'll talk about moving to Boston."

Here, with her two hands, she hurled the overnight bag into the snow at her feet. "Oh, Manny, you wouldn't move into Stockbridge because the streets are paved, so how could I ever get you to Boston? And what difference would it be in Boston anyway? You'd be just the same—you'd be worse. How could you concentrate in Boston, with all those people swarming around? There, somebody might even ask you something about your work!"

"Then maybe the best bet is to stay here."

"Even here you can't think if I so much as make toast in the kitchen—I have to catch my toast before it pops up so you won't be disturbed in the study!"

"Oh, Hopie," he said, laughing a little, "that's overdoing things. For the next thirty-five years just make your toast and forget about me."

"I *can't.*"

"Learn," he said sternly.

"No!" Picking up the bag, she turned and started down the driveway. Lonoff closed the door. I watched from the window to see that she stayed on her feet. The snow had been banked so high by the town plow the night before that when she turned into the road she immediately passed out of sight. But then, of course, she wasn't very big to begin with.

Lonoff was at the hall closet, wrestling with his overshoes.

"Would you like me to come along? To help?" I asked.

"No, no. I can use the exercise after that egg." He stamped his feet on the floor in an attempt to save himself from having to bend over again to get the boots on right. "And you must have things to write down. There's paper on my desk."

"Paper for what?"

"Your feverish notes." He pulled a large, dark, belted coat—not *quite* a caftan—from the closet and I helped him into it. Pressing a dark hat over his bald head, he completed the picture of the chief rabbi, the archdeacon, the magisterial high priest of perpetual sorrows. I handed him his scarf, which had fallen out of a coat sleeve onto the floor. "You had an earful this morning."

I shrugged. "It wasn't so much."

"So much as what, last night?"

"Last night?" Then does he know all I know? But what *do* I know, other than what I can imagine?

"I'll be curious to see how we all come out someday. It could be an interesting story. You're not so nice and polite in your fiction," he said. "You're a different person."

"Am I?"

"I should hope so." Then, as though having concluded administering my rites of confirmation, he gravely shook my hand. "Which way did she go on the road? To the left?"

"Yes. Down the mountain."

He found his gloves in his pocket and after a quick glance at his watch opened the front door. "It's like being married to Tolstoy," he said, and left me to make my feverish notes while he started off after the runaway spouse, some five minutes now into her doomed journey in search of a less noble calling.

ABOUT THE AUTHOR

Philip Roth was born in New Jersey in 1933. He studied literature at Bucknell University and the University of Chicago. His first book, *Goodbye, Columbus*, won the National Book Award for Fiction in 1960. He has lived in Rome, London, Chicago, New York City, Princeton, and New England. Since 1955, he has been on the faculties of the University of Chicago, Princeton University, and the University of Pennsylvania, where he is now Adjunct Professor of English. He is also General Editor of the Penguin Books series "Writers from the Other Europe." Recently he has been spending half of each year in Europe, traveling and writing.